LIVIN' AIN'T FOREVER

LIVIN' AIN'T FOREVER

by

Ryan Bodie

Dales Large Print Books
Long Preston, North Yorkshire,
BD23 4ND, England.

British Library Cataloguing in Publication Data.

Bodie, Ryan
    Livin' ain't forever.

    A catalogue record of this book is
    available from the British Library

    ISBN   978-1-84262-716-7 pbk

First published in Great Britain in 2008 by Robert Hale Limited

Copyright © Ryan Bodie 2008

Cover illustration © Gordon Crabb by arrangement with
Alison Eldred

Published in Large Print 2009 by arrangement with
Robert Hale Ltd.

Dales Large Print is an imprint of Library Magna Books Ltd.

Printed and bound in Great Britain by
T.J. (International) Ltd., Cornwall, PL28 8RW

CHAPTER 1

THE STONE CAGE

Amongst the few luxuries the inmates of Sharrastone Prison were permitted, was their 'swamp juice'. A blend of swamp water and molasses, the concoction had a pleasant, distinctive taste, and after enough years inside a con could believe his swamp juice was the most important luxury in life – next to his tobacco.

So it was hardly surprising that violence erupted when Buffalo Joe upset Cowboy Jones's juice-can at the start of the mid-morning break. Whether it was intentional or not didn't signify. Cowboy simply emitted an enraged roar and kicked Buffalo in the leg, then knocked the prison cap off his ugly head with a backhander. Response was swift and vicious when Buffalo retaliated with a brutal forearm jolt to the face. Within moments a mob of excited convicts was milling around the brawlers while yard boss Zane and his baton-swinging bulls attempted to cleave their way through to break it up.

Yet even as he powered through the surging mass of humanity, the veteran Zane could see the combatants were causing one another but minor damage, missing far more frequently than they connected with their wild swings, burning up most of their energy cursing.

'I hit my old lady harder than that,' Zane panted to a brother guard. And he wasn't joking. Hitting people was such an in-grained habit for the scarred boss of the big yard he found he couldn't stop even when he got home.

'You'd have to wonder what breed of clown would risk a week in The Hole just to tip over another clowns juice, wouldn't you, boss?' a burly junior guard panted, shoul-dering a cursing convict from his path. 'I don't figure it.'

The answer would strike both men too late. The ruckus between Buffalo and Cowboy was merely a diversion. The real action was about to erupt in back of the rusted iron bulk of the machine shop in a secluded corner of the quarry yard known as the West Forty.

The ruckus over the swamp juice had been staged to draw off the guards. Buffalo Joe and Cowboy Jones might each pull a day or two in The Hole for their efforts, but would be compensated in tobacco and illicit whiskey for their trouble. Their only regret would be missing the long-awaited clash between, Ford Gabriel and Reece Wallace.

Reece Wallace was the iron-fisted champ of Sharrastone. Two hundred pounds of sinew, muscle and vicious temper, he was the terror of the inmates. At least half the guards were also scared of him, to their shame. The only hope any new con had of getting along with Wallace was by acknowledging his authority from the outset, and from there on, jumping when he said jump.

The old stagers of the pen believed only a fool or somebody with an overblown notion of his own fighting ability would go out of his way to treat Wallace like a bum – as Gabriel had just done.

Some inmates had slotted Gabriel down in the simply wild and loco category in his early days behind bars. But after the new con had taken on three of the toughest inmates in the place, and won, the wise heads agreed that maybe he'd earned the right to be reclassified.

Nobody now doubted Gabriel was one tough *hombre*. Yet even though this showdown had been planned for a week, there wasn't one dollar of gambling money or can of swamp juice riding on his broad shoulders in wagers that day. The reason was simple. Everyone figured Wallace was so enraged by the way Gabriel had been goading him leading up to the showdown, that the king of the cons would not be content just to whip Gabriel today. He'd most likely try to kill him.

Gabriel stripped to the waist beneath a scorching sun.

He was deeply tanned from weeks of work down in the rock yard with a thirty-pound mallet, 'making little rocks out of big ones'. Youthfully muscled with powerful arms, Gabriel had a face that was part boy with wide-set eyes under a banner of unruly brown hair – and part veteran with square-jawed features and the look of a man who would never take a backward step.

The four senior cons delegated to witness the fight were beginning to wonder where Wallace had gotten to, when the man suddenly stepped out from the machine shop.

With the sounds of the phony Buffalo Joe-Cowboy Jones clash rising and falling in the background, Wallace strode directly towards Gabriel with big black boots crushing the gravel beneath his weight.

Wallace was doing a life stretch for murder, while Gabriel had fetched a mere twelve months for horse stealing. This showdown was seen as a clash between the undisputed king of the toughest prison in south-west Texas, and a young pretender who belonged to the short-term breed of inmate here whom the old-timers rated as 'visitors', thereby occupying a much lower status scale.

No short-termer had ever even come close to besting Wallace before. Nor any veteran, for that matter.

Gabriel's features were blank as he cocked his fists and waited for the bigger man to come to him. Wallace didn't delay, was not one to waste words. He hadn't even bothered to remove his coarse denim shirt. The bare-knuckle boss of Sharrastone's brawling cons didn't expect this showdown to last long enough to make stripping down worthwhile.

Gabriel broke his nose with the first punch.

The blow was so explosively fast Wallace had no hope of avoiding it. Blood splashed down upon his shirt while his eyes – as deep-set and pitiless as an Apache wardlord's – snapped wide momentarily to betray a rare flicker of total surprise.

Next instant that look vanished and Wallace was surging forwards into the attack with both iron fists pistoning into his adversary, instantly demonstrating he was not simply big and powerful but also a highly skilled boxer and astonishingly light on his feet.

It was like trying to stand off a tornado.

In mere moments Gabriel had one closed eye and a loose tooth, with already visible bruising showing out clearly upon chest and arms as he stood toe to toe with the hardest man he'd ever faced.

He was getting hurt, yet was hurting right back. Really hurting.

Wallace could scarce believe how hard he was being hit, for although Gabriel weighed but one-eighty he hit like a man a hundred pounds heavier. Part of this punching power was attributable to natural strength but mostly stemmed from the fierce fires that burned in the younger con's belly.

Always proddy and never afraid to mix it when the occasion warranted, Gabriel's temperament had undergone a dramatic turn for the worse since being flung into Sharrastone for a crime he didn't commit. While another might have been crushed by such a miscarriage of justice, Gabriel had reacted more like a trapped dog wolf – snarling, brawling and incurring every penalty the pen could dish out, yet somehow never seeming

12

to learn from his mistakes.

Warden Cox had dubbed him a hardhead following his first brawl, and he had more than lived up that name in the months since.

Wallace suddenly changed tactics, dropped his hands and dived forwards. He seized Gabriel about the middle in a wrestler's grip and attempted to hurl him to the ground. Ford's right knee whipped up. Wallace went white with agony as the knee slammed into his groin. Gasping and spitting froth, he attempted to apply a hammerlock hold but instead had his head snapped back by a truly brutal forearm jolt to the face.

The onlookers could scarce believe it when they saw Wallace's tree-trunk legs begin to buckle. Gabriel could. He'd landed a similar blow on Hooks Willigan his first week inside and that con had had trouble counting as high as ten ever since. He knew his man was hurt and ruthlessly set out to capitalize. A barrage of pistoning punches softened up the bigger man even further, and Gabriel now knew he was going to win.

Closing in, he applied a flying mare wrestling hold which flipped his adversary over his right hip to smash into a wall. The wall did not give but Wallace's massive bulk did. He crashed heavily to ground, one booted foot briefly stuttering before his whole body went still.

Reece Wallace was all through but Ford Gabriel was not.

He knew Wallace would have killed him, given half a chance. He wasn't about to go that far. But it was an unwritten rule in grim Sharrastone that whenever you whipped a man you made sure you did such a thorough job he'd never want to face you again.

Staggering a little now, chest heaving, Gabriel sucked in three huge breaths before advancing upon the prostrate figure, with nobody moving to stop him.

His first vicious kick set the huge body rolling. He went quickly after him but barely had time to raise his boot a second time before three guards arrived in a rush to slap him in irons and drag him off to The Hole.

After the dust settled Wallace was loaded upon a stretcher and carted off to the prison infirmary. Gabriel learned later that the doc worked on the man two hours and put twenty stiches into him. Upon hearing this the battered victor grinned like a dog wolf.

The medico didn't visit The Hole. No visitors of any stripe were allowed down there, not even to patch up the man who could now lay claim to the unofficial title,

King of Sharrastone.

From that day on, there wasn't a single guard, con, dog boy, trusty or hard-bitten lifer within those walls not prepared to acknowledge young Gabriel as the new *numero uno* of one of Texas's most notorious prisons.

Yet late that night when a Hole guard broke the rule of silence to whisper through the door slit of Gabriel's cage, 'Great work, Gabriel, that big bastard's had it comin',' he drew an unexpected response.

'Get away from my door, you blue-bellied toady! I don't need you sucking up to me. I don't need nobody!'

'Hardhead bastard,' the man complained to his relief sentry later. 'Well, if that's the way he wants it, that's how he'll get it. He wants nobody, so that's the way it will be.'

'Don't need anybody!' Gabriel muttered over and over as he paced his cage of stone. And although honestly believing he had nobody who really cared whether he lived or died, he was wrong. For travelling steadily towards the brooding bulk of Sharrastone Jail that very night was somebody he really did need, although he didn't know it yet.

The lone rider with the rocky jaw represented something which Gabriel hated even worse than he did Sharrastone Pen.

It was called American Justice.

The marshal boiled coffee and tore off a chunk of stale pone bread with strong teeth. He used sorghum to sweeten the black brew in his coffee mug then placed a strip of dried jerky upon the bread. Yet it was still hard tack, rough chow not even as good as that served to the con artists, rustlers, killers, stage agents, backshooters and thieves whom he dispatched to Texas's various state prisons on a regular basis.

But inconvenience never bothered Marshal McTigue. He had no taste for creature comforts and found that rough living and hard tack kept him fit and lean as a timberline wolf.

The sparse meal completed, the lawman got his bedroll and toted it off a hundred yards into the surrounding dark brush, where he stretched out to rest. One of the many rules he lived by out on the trails was never sleep right where you eat. He believed that it was all his many rules, habits, tricks and subterfuges which had kept him alive in a job which took him into the wildest and most remote corners of the Lone Star State on the trail of her most dangerous sons.

The lawman was scarred head to toe from

his war against the hellions, and morosely believed that someday one of that yellow-eyed outlaw breed would likely get lucky and kill him.

But until then he would hound them relentlessly to the courts, the prisons and the gallows. He would remain true to the only real mistress he'd ever known. Justice.

Waiting for sleep the lawman briefly reflected on justice and a trouble-prone young hothead named Ford Gabriel, until cobwebs filled his head.

He slept undisturbed beneath the holy stars of old Texas. While fifty miles further along the trail he was following, four hundred and eighty-five caged men slept restlessly in chains behind impenetrable stone walls, and knew, even in their dreams, that they were caged.

Like savage beasts.

Six paces forward and six paces back. The floor was like ice.

The guard he'd bad-mouthed had subsequently returned with others and they'd taken his clothing and mattress away. The underground cell which had been hacked out of solid bluestone twenty feet below Cell Block 7 was like an icehouse. When he touched his drinking mug his fingers stuck to it. His skin was puckered and felt like frozen leather to his touch.

'You'll learn, tough monkey!' a disembodied voice taunted from the other side of the door to his black pit in hell. Just on account you whipped Wallace don't mean you can treat us like dirt. You'll beg before you're through down here. Then you'll get your stuff back – mebbe!'

Gabriel knew he could well die of the cold, hunger, or the beatings that were mandatory in The Hole. He might perish from any number of causes. But the one thing he knew for certain sure, he would never beg for his stuff back. He would die first – a dozen times over.

Time passed.

How much time, he never knew.

He realized they'd skipped bringing him a meal when he heard the faint clinking of tinware and caught the scent of coffee being served to other solitary inmates.

He knew what they were trying to do, and why. In whipping Wallace he had suddenly clawed his way to top of the heap in Sharrastone's criminal hierarchy. He was the new power to be reckoned with. The bulls wanted to curb that power because they feared it.

He'd expected some punishment following the brawl, but they were handing him something extra. Had he lost he suspected he might now be sipping hot coffee.

The saying, 'nobody loves a loser', did not apply here with the guards. Losers were OK by them. It was the winners they feared. Winners attracted admirers and supporters about them and got to wield real power, which in time might threaten the guards themselves.

Dawn came with an almost imperceptible lightening of the total darkness. Gabriel broke the ice from the water bucket, washed his face and fingered his hair back into some semblance of neatness.

'Die, you bastards!' he whispered as boots went by. He didn't say it aloud because each time you broke your silence here they handed you an extra twenty-four hours.

His face broke into a cold, wolf grin. He would survive, he assured himself. He would get to swing a hammer in the rock yard again and would bide his time getting quits with The Hole guards. There wasn't much left here other than getting square...

Hours drifted by and gradually the cell warmed just a little. The prisoner continued pacing until he was reeling with exhaustion, and only then lay upon the cold floor and slept.

Mostly when he dreamed in Sharrastone they were dreams with bars and walls and leg-irons in them some place. But this dream was of his younger days when he was free to ride any place he wanted, called no man master, paid for his own whiskey and slept wherever he pleased.

To awake and find himself still in The Hole at Sharrastone Pen was a cruel and bitter disappointment.

On his feet, he moved to the door and listened intently. Once a man became accustomed to penitentiary sounds he could figure what time it was simply by what he heard, even down here in The Hole. He heard the distant whispering of hundreds of boots against stone, a faint metallic clashing that was the noise of tin trays, mugs and plates being employed. Then a faint siren. The midday meal. It was hard to believe that twenty feet above by some sixty west, brilliant sunshine was pouring down into the rock yard adjacent to the mess hall.

A further hour dragged by before he heard steps approach, followed by the grating sound of a key in the door.

Head guard Zane stood beneath the sickly

20

passageway light bundled up in a long, heavy greatcoat with a warm muffler twisted about his neck. His boots had rubber soles an inch thick. The bastard! The man studied Gabriel in a curious, half-amused way.

'What other crimes did you commit, Gabriel?' he smirked. 'That you never told us about, I mean?'

Gabriel eyed him suspiciously.

'What are you talking about?'

'As if you ain't in enough trouble here already, now they got serious law showing up here looking for you. Looks to me like they've caught up on something else you done, tough monkey.'

'Important law?'

'McTigue.'

'Marshal McTigue?'

'That's the party. I can tell you that when a man gets that bloodhound camped on his trail he might as well throw in his hand altogether. The game is over for him.'

'Are you saying McTigue's here to see me?'

'As if you didn't figger he'd show sooner or later. I'll be interested to find out what else McTigue's got to hang around your neck, tough monkey. All right, Jackson!'

A guard appeared toting Gabriel's boots and clothes. 'Am I supposed to get dressed

21

before this McTigue comes down?' Gabriel asked.

'Oh, he ain't coming down here. I mean, he's a tolerable tough-looking lawman, but he could catch a chill.'

'You mean I'm to go up and see him?' He couldn't hide his astonishment. He'd never once heard of any con being released from The Hole until he'd served his full time. Not for any reason.

Zane nodded and the guard threw him his clothes. When he was dressed, six of them fell in around him and marched him upstairs to the warden's office. It was a warm day but Gabriel still felt cold. And his single thought was – what more could the bastards do to him?

CHAPTER 2

RIDIN' FREE

'Your prison record stinks, Gabriel!' was the marshal's brusque greeting.

'Nothing on God's green earth stinks worse than a system that can put an innocent man into prison in the first place, McTigue. So, before you go sniffing about and holding your ugly nose, take a whiff of your own backyard!'

'Gabriel!' chided the warden, a fat and dithery man who appeared constantly bewildered to find himself bossing one of the toughest penal institutions in Texas. 'That's no way to address a United States marshal. Have a care or I'll slap another week on to your term in solitary.'

'Let him talk,' insisted the marshal. 'My main reason for being here is to listen to what he has to say. He arched a brow at the tall prisoner who stood flanked by two of the biggest guards in the prison. 'I'm told you racked up a big victory here yesterday, Gabriel?'

'Do they have US marshals running around checking on jailhouse brawls now?'

Gabriel knew he might attract an even longer spell in The Hole by smart-mouthing a marshal, yet couldn't hold back. In his eyes, this lawman represented the system which had enabled him to be arrested, charged, tried and convicted for a crime of which he was innocent.

Brutes like the husky yard bulls here were not his real enemies. But this gaunt-featured man with the Colt on his hip and the star on his vest was the real and powerful foe to be hated and mistrusted.

Yet he still didn't know what the hell McTigue wanted with him.

The US marshal rested a ham on the deep window recess which overlooked the rock yard where sweating convicts were smashing, harrowing and loading granite under a broiling sun. He appeared relaxed yet intent as he folded his arms and fixed the prisoner with a flint eye.

'No, I'm not here to debate your prison record, Gabriel. Just couldn't help commenting, I guess.'

'So why are you here? The real reason, that is.'

Warden Cox sighed and lowered his plump butt into his chair. He liked his inmates to make a good impression upon visiting dignitaries, and Marshal McTigue ranked highly in that category. But he feared this prisoner would treat this impressive lawman the way he did everybody else. Like dirt.

'He's just a hardhead, Marshal. What else can you expect of the breed?'

'A man needs a hard head here just to stay alive,' Gabriel growled. 'Well, McTigue, I'm still waiting. What brings you all the way down from the Rio here to Sharrastone?'

'I want to talk about Coronado.'

Gabriel's face twitched. Coronado was the big Rio Grande town where he'd been arrested. Most memories of that place were bitter, except one. That exception was maybe the best memory he'd ever had.

'What the hell for?' he demanded. 'Maybe you conniving badge-packers have dreamed up some crooked, lying way to lengthen my stretch? Is that it?'

The lawman remained unruffled.

'Tell me about Coronado, Gabriel. I wasn't there at the time, like you know. I'd like to hear the story from you personal.'

'I told the court everything. They found me guilty. So what's the point?'

'You were found guilty based upon the weight of evidence presented against you.'

'False evidence. Lies.'

'So, you can tell me the truth then, Gabriel. I've just spent a week in Coronado. Checking on you, mainly. I've heard everybody's story first hand, but yours. What have you got to lose, man?'

Gabriel was riddled with suspicion. He regarded the entire Coronado episode as something best forgotten, even if he knew he would surely never forget it himself? But if

25

the Coronado court had found him guilty as charged, what was to be gained hauling over the cold ashes of it all now? And why should McTigue believe anything he might say now when nobody else had done so before?

Yet on the other side of that coin he recalled there had always been something about this formidable peace officer which he found encouraging, maybe even sincere. He'd always heard McTigue described as 'straight as a string', and had tended to believe it. So, he considered that big question again: what did he have to lose?

Maybe nothing.

'All right. Just what is it you want to know?' he asked grudgingly.

'You claimed at your trial you'd been framed,' the lawman responded briskly, leaning back. 'What made you come to that conclusion?'

Gabriel sighed. He'd repeated the story more often than he could recollect but it hadn't done him one lick of good.

But again – what did he really have to lose?

'I was breaking wild horses out along Trib Creek' he stated, massaging his jaw where one of Wallace's powerhouse punches had crashed through his defence. 'I had eleven mustangs penned in a brush corral. I rolled into my blankets one night and got awaked at dawn by the Coronado law led by Sheriff Champion. A blood horse had been stolen from Daybreak Ranch. So they inspected my cavvy, and sure enough, this horse I'd never seen before was found amongst them. Somebody had dirtied it up some and run him through the brush beforehand to make it look like I was trying to disguise it so's it wouldn't be identified by anybody just passing by.' He shrugged. 'They arrested me.'

'Following a big fight,' Cox said prissily, tapping Gabriel's file which lay on his desk.

'Wouldn't you start fighting back if somebody tried to frame you, fat man?' Gabriel snapped.

Furiously, Cox began scribbling on a pad. Gabriel reckoned he was making a list of new offences to charge him with later. He didn't give a damn ... or so he wanted to believe.

The marshal said crisply, 'You alleged in court you were incriminated as part of a plot hatched up by the combined Vega and Moneros families in order to get rid of you. Can you tell me exactly why you made that claim?'

'You know, badgeman, I've a powerful feeling you already know everything that happened or was said at that farce of a trial already. What good will all this do?'

'I told you, Gabriel. I have good reason to want to hear it all from your own mouth.'

Gabriel sighed gustily. Seemed it might be simpler just to go along with the badge-packer than try to argue.

He talked fast, wanting only to get it over with now.

'I was keeping company with Señorita Carmelita Vega at that time, and her family got sore about it. The Vegas are one of the oldest families in Coronado, rich Mex aristos who see all gringos as trash. Well, the Vega clan didn't want their daughter stepping out with my kind, and for more than one good reason. First, they saw me as a roughneck with no future. But far more important, they'd arranged to have her betrothed to a rich, older greaser by the name of Zebulon Moneros who owns the Hacienda, the finest cattle spread within a hundred miles of Coronado.'

'And her family naturally figured your association with their daughter might jeopardize her romance with this Señor Moneros?' the lawman surmised.

'Sure did.' He shrugged. 'They warned me off, then tried to buy me off. When nothing worked they sicced a bunch of roughcases onto me. But I worked them over with a stockwhip and promised to do the same to Rodrigo Vega next time our paths crossed. Next day I found a horse I'd never seen before in my corral and within a week I was sentenced to a year in Sharrastone for horse-stealing. Now, if there's nothing else–'

'A likely story!' sniffed the warden, who would have said more but the marshal's scowl warned him to silence.

But what was the veteran manhunter really thinking at that moment?

A defiant Gabriel tried to convince himself he didn't give a rap what was going on behind McTigues pensive scowl. But he was soon destined to find out when the lawman began firing a whole barrage of questions at him in rapid succession. The badge-packer wanted to hear every detail and jotted down notes in an official-looking notebook as he talked. He frequently paused to chew the end of his pencil while studying the prisoner with a rare intensity, which Gabriel found both puzzling and off-putting. Just what was McTigue really trying to get out of him?

Wearily and with increasing irritation he eventually convinced himself the man was here simply to garner added evidence against him in order to lengthen his sentence.

29

He'd never been more wrong in his life.

Marshal McTigue sat pondering in total silence for several minutes after hearing the prisoner's response to his final question. He puffed on his pipe and occasionally scratched his head.

Time passed and an increasingly tetchy Gabriel was on the brink of losing his temper when McTigue suddenly slapped his thigh, got up and crossed the room with right hand extended.

'Let me be first to congratulate you, Gabriel. As of this moment you are a free man.'

For a moment, Gabriel's face suffused with astonishment and delight. But no longer than that, as the suspicion hit that he was being made the butt of some twisted and cruel joke. He'd never cold-cocked a federal lawman before but that was about to change. Fast.

'You son of a bitch!' he snarled, and hauled his right arm back ready to swing, only to have himself claimed from behind by the alert bulls. In the noisy scuffle that ensued the marshal backed away far enough to enable him to tug something from inside his shirt which he then waved before the struggling Gabriel's face.

It appeared to be some official-looking

document tied with a strip of pink ribbon, and this riled him even more. So he went on struggling – until the lawman lost his temper

'Damnit, if you'll stop acting like one of your mustangs a moment, Gabriel, you will take a look at this – otherwise I'll have to steady you down with a gun barrel!'

'What the hell is it?' Gabriel panted, unable to break free of strong arms. 'A death sentence, maybe?'

'It's a writ of habeas corpus authorizing me to release the body, namely yours, from durance. It's signed by Coronado's Judge Osgood and is notarized by the Chief Marshal.'

Gabriel had stopped struggling – for the moment. His brow furrowed suspiciously. 'Habeas corpus? Ain't that the hoopla you lawdogs trot out when you're arresting somebody?'

'Usually, yes. But in this case it's used in a reverse although quite proper and legal manner. Warden, I'm sure your experience makes you familiar with this procedure when a man can be officially released even though he's not actually pardoned?'

'Certainly, Marshal.' Cox attempted to smile at his ex-prisoner but Gabriel's scowl intimidated him.

Gabriel himself was still a long way from

31

smiling. Yet at least he didn't appear ready to wreak havoc any longer. He ceased struggling altogether and shook his head uncertainly. 'You mean this ... this isn't some dirty lawman's game, McTigue?'

'I don't play games with men's feelings, Gabriel.'

'But, I just don't figure...'

'Several months after you had raised such a ruckus about being framed and all the rest of it at your trial,' McTigue explained, the Chief Marshal authorized me to conduct a complete investigation into the whole matter which unfortunately for you, I was too busy to undertake until just recently But I studied the trial transcript at great length then set about interrogating the various witnesses involved. It wasn't long until irregularities began to appear. Some things simply did not add up–'

'Are you saying you realized people had lied at the trial?' Gabriel cut in.

The lawman nodded. 'Too many people lied and in time I came to suspect the Moneros bunch may have been the worst offenders. In the end I had sufficient evidence to present to a Special Board of Inquiry which eventually led to a full re-opening of your case before Judge Osgood, who heard all the fresh evidence and finally felt confident enough to bring down a verdict of "not proven".'

'Does that mean innocent?' Gabriel demanded.

'It means what it says. It's an old Scottish law. It means that while there may be some doubt concerning innocence or guilt, there is insufficient evidence to confirm guilt, and therefore the person charged must, under law, be set free.'

And he was.

Yet despite the fact that he found himself presented with an official document declaring him a free citizen under Texas law, and then had a US marshal personally supervise his release and arrange to have his horse brought in from the Prison Department's range, Ford Gabriel didn't really believe any of it until several hours later when he found himself riding unchallenged through the forbidding gates of Sharrastone pen with the afternoon sun in his eyes.

Cox and McTigue looked down from the high parapets of the prison to witness the release of a man who, until that day, had seemed at risk of parleying a one-year sentence into something far longer due to rebellious behaviour and a seeming indifference to his fate.

They'd returned his clothes, and though his jacket appeared a little tight across the shoulders and his hat the worse for wear, Ford Gabriel, ex-con, managed to project a jaunty picture as he rode off down the trail without once glancing back.

Prison boss and flinty marshal watched him travel out past the giant cottonwood to the crossroads where five trails intersected. They noted that he didn't even hesitate before selecting the south-eastern road marked by a sign which read:

CORANADO 75 MILES

'A born hardhead,' remarked Warden Cox.

Marshal McTigue nodded but did not comment. He knew all about the hard-headed breed. He'd been often accused of belonging to it himself.

Gabriel rode easy in the saddle, inhaling so deeply of the fragrances of the high country that he was starting to make himself feel dizzy.

No sour cooking smells or pensive stink of long-unwashed bodies. No clink of steel manacles or the ringing chime of hammers busting rocks. Out here there was only bird-song with easy breezes blowing down a mountain valley so gently they touched a man's face like a kiss ... like the kiss of a dark-eyed beauty with a blood-red rose in her hair.

Cottonwood trees along a stream were lush with summer green ... goldenrod yellow on either side of this horse trail, which wound leisurely over hills and valleys into the distance.

He passed by an abandoned farm where neglected orchards sagged under the burden of ripened fruits. Grapes showed a dusty purple through the leaves of a low, bushy vineyard while scarlet strings of chili hung from the porch roof of an old ranch house set far hack off the trail.

Peace, tranquility, beauty. All were to be encountered along this sweep of trail. They soothed and pleased the rider of the big brown horse ... and kept his thoughts from leaping ahead to whatever it was he might get to see and feel when he eventually rode down the main street of Coronado.

The horse was beginning to play out as the sun slid down the western sky, so he began looking about for somewhere to camp.

Some place quiet and peaceful sounded just fine, for he might not find similar conditions awaiting him when he reached where he was headed.

He hoped she would be happy to see him again even if her family's reaction would surely be just the opposite.

The flame of sunset was fading off the hilltops and dusk was creeping through the sycamores fringing the little creek when he finally found the spot he was searching for.

He entered a natural clearing and swung down. The horse blew loudly through its nostrils and shook its head-harness wearily. Like any true horseman, he attended to his mount first, off-saddling, watering, brushing and feeding the animal before attending to his own wants.

Soon he had coffee going. He drank a mugful as he played the stream with a small line fashioned from twine and a bent pin with a little pone bread for bait.

The fish he finally landed was small, but plump and tender. He cooked it with wild onions and ate it with more coffee. Cleaning his utensils with creek sand, he packed them away before stretching out before the fire with his saddle for a pillow to smoke the last cigarette of the best day of his life.

Bright stars wheeled overhead. It was now less than a day's ride to the Rio Grande and Coronado. Maybe Carmelita was watching these same jewelled stars ... and wondered if she'd yet heard the news. He frowned and sat up.

Would it prove good news for her? Maybe during his imprisonment she might have made up her mind to marry Zebulon Moneros ... might even be already married...?

He dismissed that thought instantly, and instead tried to picture her excited to hear the news of his unexpected release.

His thoughts drifted back to when they'd first met. They were instantly attracted despite the adverse reactions of friends and family Particularly the family. Yet they began keeping company right off despite all opposition. For they were young and it was springtime on the Rio Grande, and what law said they couldn't walk out together if they wanted?

They soon found out why when the Vega and Moneros families joined forces and began mounting pressure to force the horsebreaker to quit town, culminating in his conviction for horse theft and eventual transportation to Sharrastone.

His expression grew sombre by the fire glow. Had theirs been real love or merely an innocent friendship? He saw it as something far deeper and stronger, but maybe he'd been mistaken? He could not be sure, yet would still make directly for Coronado by the shortest possible route. But whether he was driven by the desire to see Carmelita Vega again, or simply to flaunt his new freedom before the people who'd railroaded him into prison, he could not be certain.

Yet lying back with hands locked behind his head, waiting for sleep, he knew one thing for certain. Carmelita had never once left his mind during his term of imprisonment. Not a single day had passed when he didn't think of her. And there had never been anyone in his old, freewheeling life who'd had that effect.

Maybe it was true love after all? Stranger things had happened.

Tomorrow will tell...' he murmured drowsily And was closing his eyes when somewhere close by in the velvet Texas night he heard the unmistakable sound of a boot brushing against rock...

CHAPTER 3

YOU'VE BEEN WARNED!

Don Zebulon Moneros wasn't by habit an early riser. But today was different. The maidservant had awakened him to inform there was an important message concerning the gringo, Gabriel. So the rich man complainingly got himself dressed, ordered a goblet of Madeira to help get rid of the cobwebs, then made his way downstairs.

The don made an impressive sight as he descended the richly carpeted staircase. He was a handsome forty-year-old man who was still impressive and vigorous enough in appearance for few people to notice the wide silk cummerbund he'd lately taken to wearing in order to conceal the first signs of a paunch.

King of the finest range of cattle country along this stretch of the Rio Grande, Moneros was the perfect example of somebody who'd always had too much, too soon. Too much wealth, status and women –

and far too much fine food and splendid wines.

And of course, power.

Where so many of his original countrymen had seen their cattle empires engulfed by America's headlong western expansion, Moneros by contrast had proved to be smart and ruthless enough to hang on to his original kingdom of grass and cattle and had even eventually expanded it to achieve its current power and prestige as the finest outfit within one hundred miles – on either side of the Rio Grande.

Around Coronado there were now any number of small American ranchers struggling to survive simply because Moneros's Hacienda Rancho reared the finest cattle, secured the best markets and always wielded the greatest strength and power.

Many a newly arrived settler complained that it was not right that a Mexican should be in a position to lord it over Americans. Yet if Moneros heard such complaints it only served to make him that much more determined to grow still larger, stronger and richer.

Rivals could gripe all they wanted. He had the power and only Old Man Death would ever cause him to relinquish it. Power was the name of the game and the don played with an expert's touch.

A maidservant bowed low as he reached the foot of the stairs but Moneros appeared not to even see the girl. His gleaming black boots were silent upon thick carpet as he passed through the tall French doors which gave onto the terrace.

The Moneros mansion stood on a hill overlooking the Rio Grande to the north side, with mile upon mile of lush cattle grazelands on the Mexican side. It was a superb Spanish building with wrought-iron balconies and vast, tree-shaded courtyards. Fountains tinkled in the courts and armies of servants maintained it all in immaculate order.

At the base of the hill nestled a grubby little scatter of daub huts where his American and Mexican cow-herders lived.

The don's father had taught him all the important laws of the ruling classes before passing on, one of which was basically to keep the hired help hungry, an edict which Zebulon Moneros observed strictly.

A powerful, squat figure mounted the marble steps as Moneros appeared upon the balustrade. Chantaro did not appear either hungry or ill-treated. But then, he was no lowly *vaquero* or day labourer either. His role here was that of personal bodyguard. Chantaro frequently ate at the don's table and slept in a chair outside his locked bedroom door during troubled times when danger might threaten.

The don saw to it that a man with such an important responsibility had the best of everything to keep him fit, strong and satisfied.

Chantaro doffed his black sombrero. 'Good morning, *patrón*.'

Like Moneros himself the husky guntipper had but a slight accent. The American influence had penetrated every level of Coronado life. Traditionalists such as the Vegas aristocrats might still exhibit strong Spanish accents but such things were of little importance to Moneros. He saw no virtue in anything which didn't produce actual profit.

'What is the message?' Moneros was sampling his Madeira.

'Gabriel is coming back to Coronado.'

'The deputies encountered him?'

'Encountered is the word, *patrón*. It appears Gabriel got the best of them and made them appear fools.'

'How could such a thing happen?'

'They will not say much, Don Zebulon. But I gather they attempted to jump him in a camp in the hills and he turned the tables on them.

'*Madre de Dios!* Such incompetence. I should have sent you.'

'Perhaps. In any case, *patrón*, they're back. They claim Gabriel intends to take up here where he left off a year ago. He also spoke of squaring accounts with those he claimed framed him into prison…'

'Does Vega know of this?'

'I know not.'

'Then go inform him.'

Chantaro saluted briskly. 'On my way, Don Zebulon. Anything else?"

The don scowled thinking now of Antonio Vega's daughter. The Señorita Carmelita was one of the very *few* things in his life the don genuinely desired, yet had so far had been unable to acquire. And 'desire' 'was the word. The don had never understood love but knew all about lust and desire. For too long he'd wanted to possess Carmelita Vega's lithe young womanhood. He wanted her and was even preparing to make her his legally wedded Donna Moneros in order to have her, if that was what it took. His plans had the full support of the Vega family who stood to make impressive financial gains with the official linking of the families. Yet

Carmelita was, at best, lukewarm about the upcoming nuptials.

The don's expression darkened at that thought.

She had been far warmer towards him a year ago before that troublemaker Gabriel first showed upon the streets of Coronado, he reflected bitterly.

There had been no other potential suitors for her hand back then, while the Vega family had done all they could to persuade their daughter to accept the don's offer of marriage. But a swaggering Yankee tough in a red shirt had walked into her life and Carmelita Vega had never been the same since.

Of course dramatic steps had been taken eventually by both involved families to rid themselves of the troublesome Texan. As a result of Gabriel's imprisonment Don Moneros had made considerable progress in his courtship of Carmelita Vega during his rival's time behind bars, with wedding plans now well advanced. But then came the unforeseen investigation into the whole Gabriel matter by Marshal McTigue which had eventually overturned the findings of the court, resulting in Gabriel's unexpected release.

The big question here now was, 'Would Gabriel return to Coronado?' The answer appeared to be yes, and the don found this deeply disturbing.

Even so, the horse-buster was viewed merely as one of those irritating aspects in life which might occasionally disturb even a man of Moneros's stature – like a mosquito which interrupted his sleep.

Until word came through of the man's pending release from Sharrastone, that was. The moment the don had heard of this, the mosquito loomed as something far more irritating, even dangerous.

But he had men on his payroll accomplished at swatting such pests. A pair of this breed had been dispatched to do whatever was necessary to divert the jailbird from his plans to return to Coronado, but it seemed a big brawling horsebreaker was not always so easily diverted. This was one wasn't, at least.

He searched for a diversion from disagreeable thoughts and succeeded.

'Carmelita!'

The don rolled the name around his mouth and the old familiar fires began to burn within him. He had to have her. And soon. Nothing could be permitted to get in his way...

'Just go visit Antonio and Rodrigo Vega,' he instructed his man with sudden decisiveness.

'Inform both that I find the news of Gabriel's return to Coronado ... unsatisfactory.'

'Unsatisfactory? Will they understand your meaning, *patron?*'

'They had damned better!'

'It shall be done, Don Moneros.'

The gunman left and the don stood in the morning sunlight overlooking his rolling acres. Most days this sight made him feel like the unchallenged king of the Rio Grande. Not today. He was so accustomed to getting anything he wanted that the prospect of his marriage to Carmelita being further delayed was like acid against his teeth.

He returned inside, calling for more Madeira. His voice set off a trembling through the mansion. Whenever Don Moneros was angry, wise people had good reason to be afraid.

Gabriel left his hotel door opened while he unpacked his bed roll and possibles sack. He reckoned it would be a long time before he would feel completely comfortable sleeping behind a locked door again.

Deep down he realized he'd much rather doss down under the stars and wide open skies in all weathers – even some lonely place out along the Rio Grande or even at smelly old Dead Crow Canyon – than here at Coronado's Rio Grande Hotel.

Yet there were plenty reasons for setting up here in town, not the least of which was making sure all his many enemies knew he was back and planned to stay.

It had taken longer to get to Coronado than he'd calculated for several reasons, not the least of which had been constantly making certain nobody was dogging his steps. In the wake of his clash with the deputies the previous night, he'd had to wonder how many more 'welcome home' events might have been plotted in order to 'persuade' him to move on.

One thing was for sure. If there were others planning a hot reception for him they had best wear their fighting gear.

Next thing he was warning himself against taking too many chances – and had to smile at himself. Freedom and home were both so unexpected and exhilarating he reckoned it might be quite a time before he could settle down to an even keel and stop borrowing trouble as he was now doing.

It wasn't much of a room, just a ten-by-ten square with cracked lino on the floor and a tattered blind. The walls were adorned with a faded pink rose-patterned wallpaper he'd seen duplicated in a hundred hotel rooms across the great West. Bed, bureau, washbasin and a single rickety chair. That was it. Not luxurious by any yardstick but then no horsebreaker just released from prison expected fancy trimmings.

This would do him just fine.

He checked his appearance in the wall mirror, curious to see what changes prison had made.

He stared. He realized he looked tougher. Tougher and older.

He wouldn't turn twenty-five until next birthday, yet reckoned that the sober, sunbrowned mug staring back at him today, in this glass, looked thirty. Minimum.

And he thought, would Carmelita think he'd aged when and if she saw him?

He'd received no letters during his term in Sharrastone. He was certain her family would have prevented her writing. There was also the possibility that with him away and behind bars the girl might have come round to seeing him through her parents eyes – namely as a brawling horsebreaker with slim prospects and a genuine talent for trouble?

Maybe it was even far worse than that? It could be she was already betrothed to Don Moneros? A man didn't pick up much gossip behind the prison's high walls.

And he wondered ... if he should discover she simply was no longer interested any more, for whatever reason, would he want to stay on in Coronado?

'The hell!' he snorted aloud and, scooping up his hat, went out, banging the door behind him.

The big trouble with jail, a man had far too much time for thinking and brooding. He'd always been more a doer than a thinker. Could be it was time he slipped back into that old action mode again.

CHAPTER 4

FIRST BLOOD

In the gloomy lobby with its battered old desk, limp potted palms and a desk clerk with a two-day growth, Gabriel sighted a familiar face. The man sat slumped in a rickety chair chewing a dead match. When Ford had seen him last he'd been a poor rancher with tons of grit. He still looked poor but the gritty look appeared to be missing.

49

The man grew aware of his attention and glanced up. His eyes widened as he rose. 'Damn me if it ain't the mule man!' he grinned. 'I heard they'd sprung you but I just didn't believe it. How you travelling, Ford boy?'

Fine,' he said, and grabbed the out-stretched hand.

Jack Sibley ranched west along the Rio. Gabriel had hunted horses with him often in the surrounding hills. The two hit it off well enough. The 'mule man' tag came about when the rancher had first witnessed Ford's mule-like stubbornness in hunting a mustang mare through the wild brush country which a prairie dog would avoid. He'd wound up roping that mare only when she finally collapsed from simple exhaustion a week later.

He was that breed of wild horse hunter.

'You look kind of low,' Gabriel remarked. 'What have you been doing while I was gone?'

'Why, getting ground deeper and deeper under, I guess, Ford. Want to hear about it?'

'Some other time, Jack. I got things to do tonight. You understand?'

'Sure, sure. By gosh, but you look fit and ringy enough to lick your weight in range bulls, man. Sharrastone must have agreed with you.'

'Mebbe, but I sure didn't agree with it. Well, see you around.'

'Sure. Oh, there's just one thing.

Gabriel paused. 'Yeah?'

'Be careful.'

'Of what?'

'You know. There's them around Coronado who sure ain't happy you're back, mule man. Big people.'

'I know. But it's still a free country, ain't it?'

'Is it?'

Gabriel tossed him a half-salute and went out.

Coronado by night was something he'd pictured countless times in prison. By day it was simply a big sprawling town drowsing on the banks of the Rio but at night it took on a softer and more romantic atmosphere common to many such places of Spanish origin.

Strolling, he encountered promenading girls, some American and some Mexican, yet all uncommonly pretty to the gaze of a man just released from prison. Young men stood watching the girls parade by and he realized how innocent everyone looked. He hoped none of them ever wound up in Sharrastone. He wouldn't wish that on his worst enemy ... or would he?

He realized he'd drawn to a halt before the imposing office building of Vega and Son, Dealers. This was where Antonio Vega and his son Rodrigo conducted their cattle, sheep and horse-dealing business. The firm had other commercial interests but trading in livestock prodded their prime source of income. In his early days around Coronado Gabriel had sold Vega some of his broken mustangs. At a later time, after he'd shown interest in Carmelita Vega, young Rodrigo had warned him that if he set foot in the place again he'd take a horsewhip to him.

He grinned wryly. Maybe a stretch in Sharrastone would do that pair of money-grubbers some genuine good, he mused, moving on. His smile widened as he considered that wildly unlikely possibility. But if it did happen, then at least he'd he free to visit their sister and daughter any time he wanted.

He sobered and thought, 'Providing, of course, she is still interested.'

A man accidentally bumped him at a corner and Ford growled at him. The citizen apologized and hurried off. Passers-by watched Gabriel curiously as he tilted his hat forward and moved on. He realized he was growing touchy simply thinking about

Carmelita instead of making contact. Maybe he should deal with that?

Some time later he was standing in the shadows of a big old plane tree across the broad avenue along the river bluffs directly across from the sprawling Vega compound. Second to the Monteros headquarters of Hacienda Rancho, the Vegas' town house was the finest in the county. Double-storeyed and constructed along classical Spanish lines, it exuded taste, wealth and refinement.

He'd never been inside those massive, scrolled-iron gates and doubted he ever would. He grudgingly supposed he was impressed by it all, even if wealth and material possessions had never meant much to him. Freedom was his passion, not bricks, mortar and polished cedar furnishings.

The mansion was ablaze with lights tonight.

He knew Carmelita's window. Gazing up, he thought how ironical it was that the very first woman he'd ever loved should belong to a family which held his kind in contempt. But, of course, life could often be that way: with the sweet came the bitter. Maybe that was what made it all so interesting.

Over the space of half an hour he observed two riders and a closed carriage quitting the mansion but no sign of Carmelita. He stubbed out his thin Mexican cheroot and emerged from the shadows of the trees. As he headed back for the plaza his jaw muscles worked and deep creases lined his cheeks, sure indicators he was coming down hard on himself.

'No real sand in your craw, Gabriel,' he muttered. 'That's your big trouble. You take on a stinking jail full of guards, yet you're too yellow to march up to a front gate, slam the knocker and tell whoever answers you're here to visit with Carmelita – and right now!'

He shook his head as he rounded a corner. Of course, to do such a thing might well touch off an uproar to rival the racket down at Kitty Dechine's place on River Street on pay nights.

A more sobering consideration was that such a fool stunt might even upset Carmelita. He was certain she loved him ... but family ties were powerful in Coronado on the Rio and his romantic prospects there would still have to rate up in those handsome rooms as some place between low and zero.

Which of course he would be setting out to improve as time went by now he was back home.

He didn't bother looking too closely at

how he might get to achieve that goal.

He was more relaxed after putting himself outside a sizeable steak at a side street diner. He smoked a good cigar over his joe and was paying the check when a Vega houseboy came in and made his way directly across to his corner table.

He'd brought a note. Scented. Recognizing the handwriting, Gabriel ripped it open and scanned the brief note. It read:

Ford,
I'm so thrilled you are free again. I would love to see you but dare not try just yet, because of the family. But do please be patient and I shall get to meet you perhaps in a few days.
  Carmelita

'A hostler saw you beneath the big tree,' the messenger informed Ford. 'He told this to the *señorita* but nobody else.'

'How is she?' he asked. 'Is she well?'

'As always, Señorita Carmelita is enjoying perfect health.'

He scanned the note again. It sounded both warm and encouraging. And yet, she said she couldn't see him. Did that indicate a coolness or was it simply family pressures, as she claimed?

As though reading his thoughts, the house boy spoke up. 'There has been much discussion of your release from prison at the house, Señor Gabriel. Don Antonio and Rodgrigo are both much upset.'

'I'll wager they are. But tell me about Carmelita. I haven't heard any news. She isn't married to that rich old hog, is she?'

'Don Moneros? No, not yet. But he has been courting her persistently in your absence and many expect they may wed any day now– Who knows?'

'Uh-huh. Well, thanks a heap, *amigo.*'

He proffered a gratuity but the boy shook his head.

'I believe you are a better man than many say, *señor.* Therefore I feel it my duty to warn you that there may be great danger for you should you remain in Coronado. I-I cannot say more, but perhaps that is enough. *Adios.*'

Ford watched him disappear before lighting up a cigar and quitting the eatery. He had much to occupy his mind. The boy's warning was plainly genuine. But he refused to allow it to discourage him. For Carmelita's note had put him in high spirits. It had succeeded in dispelling those doubts which had only begun to plague him since reaching Coronado. She'd said she hoped to see him soon, but he doubted he would be able to wait very long, though he was content to leave things as they were for tonight, at least.

He figured it should prove easy enough to amuse himself at the South-western Saloon. Number one on his list would be to get to do something at last about his long, long thirst.

That big sorrel was a bucking fool. They'd warned Gabriel the stallion was mean and tricky yet typically he'd taken the challenge of the ride far too lightly.

He barely had time to fling arms protectively around his head before he struck the ground and bounced straight into the corral fence. He was lying dazed with 1,500 lbs of killer bronc rearing above him when somebody grabbed him by both ankles and hauled him out beneath the bottom railings. The horse came down with its front legs stiff as crowbars on the exact spot where he had been lying just seconds before. It screamed in frustration and attempted to savage a rancher perched on the top railing, upsetting the man's balance and causing him to crash down almost on top of Ford. He swore and shoved the man away then got to his feet. For several moments he was forced to hang onto the corral fence until the landscape ceased pitching before his eyes. He spat blood and drew his sleeve across his mouth, looking tough and resolute.

'Ready him again,' he said thickly. 'He just got lucky that time, is all.'

'Better call it quits, Ford,' advised the man who'd almost landed on him, friend Jack Sibley. 'Old Ugly's just getting his second breath but by the looks of it you don't have any wind left.'

'I said get the mongrel ready,' Gabriel snapped. 'I mean pronto!'

Corral hands hurried to do his bidding. He sounded mad yet really wasn't. He was simply having one hell of a good time here at Duncan's Horse Yards where a man could always pick up a few dollars for breaking work – if he had the guts to climb aboard one of Duncan's 'specials'.

The outsized sorrel would fetch $100 if Duncan could just get it broken, yet was worth only $15 as horsemeat if not. The brute had been at the yards almost a month now, defeating all comers.

Sibley, hard up for cash, had taken a try in the saddle first up, but had been thrown clear over the corral fence at first buck.

Gabriel, itching to get himself back into the routine which he'd missed so vitally while in prison, had lasted longer today yet had still finished up on his back.

'I can see this critter filling cans marked "Dogmeat" afore the end of the week,' Duncan sighed pessimistically as yard hands slung looped ropes and a blindfold upon the quivering sorrel. 'I guess I'll have to accept he's just plain unrideable.'

'There's no such critter,' declared Gabriel, knocking clouds of dust off his rig with his hat. He squinted at Sibley who was nursing a bruised arm. 'Just what are you doing down here anyway, Jack?' he asked curiously. 'This here is a young man's game. Matter of fact, it pays to be young and thick in the head, both.'

'Tough times, mule man,' the rancher said, inspecting his arm. He glanced up. I figure I'm through with ranching, Ford. Me and a lot of other smallholders. Looks like the army up at Fort Brent is aiming to draw up contracts for the Vegas and the Moneros ranch to supply all army beef from here on in. Them military outfits have been keeping us small operators going for years.' He winced as he prodded at his arm. 'I'm as good as broke. The ten bucks I could earn

59

for riding this monster would keep me going another couple of weeks, maybe longer.'

'Is that what you wanted to tell me last night?'

'Ulh-huh.' Sibley turned his head. We're all going to go bust if that deal goes through with the army. I'd have to sell up for a song. And I guess I don't have to tell you who is all set to snap us up?'

'The Vegas?'

'Uh-huh, got it in one. Well, looks like they got Ugly ready for you again, son. You sure you want to try again?'

With a grunt Gabriel clambered up onto the corral fence and glared at the horse. Blindfolded and well held, Old Ugly stood as docile as a pet lamb. The nostrils were flared but silent. The stallion was just waiting to be uncovered and let loose for him to explode into his whirling dervish imitation again.

Dropping lightly to ground, Gabriel crossed the yard and vaulted into the saddle, jaw set in bulldog lines, eyebrows knit in fierce concentration.

'All right – let the ugly mongrel go!'

The hands did as ordered – then ran like hell. The sorrel quivered and rolled its eyes. Then it exploded into a series of violent bucks around the corral which had the watchers cheering while Gabriel clung on for dear life.

It was a ride to watch and remember with the horse using every trick it knew to dislodge the rider who in turn simply refused to get tossed out of that saddle. Dust rose in a choking yellow cloud over the rapidly swelling crowd while the rider clocked up forty seconds – now fifty.

Ford felt as if every tooth was jarring loose, yet consoled himself that this was still more like a picnic compared to a day in rock yard in Sharrastone. He kept his saddle – and suddenly felt the animal begin to falter. He wanted to cheer. He was riding the critter to a standstill when he realized the onlookers had all quit hollering for him.

An ugly thought crossed his mind. Were they taking the horse's side? The hell with them if they were!

One final series of plunging forward bucks and Old Ugly was all through. He halted, legs spraddled, head hanging low – and Gabriel had earned his fee as he dropped to the ground on rubbery legs.

With his shirt plastered to his body with sweat he made his unsteady way across the yard towards the strangely subdued mob. Thick dust drifted in yellow tatters about the corral and it wasn't until Ford climbed out through the corral fence that he saw the reason everybody had gone so quiet.

Seated astride a seventeen-hands thoroughbred, hands crossed over the saddle pommel and staring down at him with icy arrogance, was Rodrigo Vega.

Ford halted and swabbed his face with a kerchief.

It was plain Rodrigo had grown even taller and filled out strongly since he saw him last. His moustache and goatee were neatly trimmed while the ornate sombrero would have cost thirty dollars, minimum.

Glancing at the onlookers Gabriel felt their unease and apprehension. All were aware of the bad blood between the two men. They were also familiar with Rodrigo Vega's hot temper. The way he caressed the big bullwhip coiled around his saddle pommel made them feel uneasy. They were easing back as Duncan came forward, proffering a $10 bill.

'You sure earned it, Ford,' he said, glancing up at the silent Vega. 'A great ride.'

'Give it to Jack.'

'Sibley?'

'Yeah.' Gabriel was holding Vega's stare. 'He needs it worse than me. You see, certain greedy bastards here have been trying to squeeze him off his land recently.'

Duncan stepped backwards with the bill as Rodrigo Vega arched an eyebrow at Gabriel, arrogant features showing no change at the implied insult.

Vega was a turbulent mix of hardworking businessman, dutiful son and churchgoer. As well, the man was a noted gambler, womanizer, and duellist. He was horse-crazy and was often to be seen racing down by the river with affluent companions who regarded him as their natural leader and the best man in town to have on your side. Yet overall he was far from being a popular man in Coronado despite commanding attention and respect. One of the few people who had never given him either was the broad-shouldered man standing before him now.

'So, Gabriel, you are back.'

'Seems like it.'

'You were warned to stay away and yet you chose to return.'

'That's so. I go where I please and when I want.'

'Except when behind bars for horse-stealing.'

'Except when some dirty sons of bitches framed me for something I never did and lied me into prison, you mean!'

Gabriel's manner was threatening yet the other seemed unruffled.

'You were unwise to return.'

'You don't own Coronado.'

'I own far more of it than you do, saddle bum. I have a stake in this town, something you would never understand. I have put much into Coronado but men such as yourself, all you do is take – and spoil whatever you touch!'

'Reckon we could go on like this for quite a time, Mex. But unless you've got something to say that's even halfway interesting ... I got other things to do.'

'There is something else.' Rodrigo had dismounted and was slowly uncoiling his whip.

Gabriel knew he was handy with a whip, maybe the best he'd ever encountered.

'I came searching for you to warn you to quit Coronado and never return,' Rodrigo went on.

Gabriel's eyes flared cold and hard.

'I never reckoned you smart Mex but I guess I never took you for a fool either. Until now. Nobody tells me what to do ... least of all you!'

'Why me?'

'Because I know you helped railroad me into Sharrastone, you lying, conniving bastard! You're lucky you're not in there yourself for that. But you could well be after I drum up the evidence against you I need. So now maybe you understand why?'

The Mexican drew himself up to full height. He was white with fury as he spoke. 'And you should understand I know about the note!'

Gabriel stared. 'What?'

'The house-boy was caught sneaking back in last night. Under questioning he revealed you'd been skulking about and had received a note from my sister. He was instantly dismissed, of course. I was in favour of going directly to the sheriff to charge you over your renewed harassment of my sister, but my father persuaded me to come see you personally and offer you a final chance to leave town of your own accord.'

'Harass?' Gabriel challenged. 'I've never harassed a woman in my life. That's a dirty lie – like everything else I've ever heard come out of your mouth.'

The Mexican's eyes flared wildly. You ... you dare call Rodrigo Vega a-a liar?'

'A dirty, lying scum!'

The whip leapt like a live thing and cut viciously across Gabriel's chest and arm – and he charged.

65

Confident in his power, Gabriel balanced himself then swung a solid right cross at the jaw. It missed. Rodrigo ducked beneath the blow and lashed back with a right to the mouth that had Gabriel seeing stars.

'Surprised, saddle bum?' the Mexican jeered as they circled, searching for an opening. 'Surprised that a Mexican gentlemen should be expert at your crude gringo sport of fist-fighting?'

His taunt drew no response. Ford would let his fists speak for him. Drawing the man's guard down with a feint, he switched the attack to the head. He scored with two hard left hooks before he was taken unawares by a left rip to the guts he didn't see coming.

This Mex dude really could fight!

Time to get deadly serious.

Yet even as he weaved and bobbed expertly to land finally a solid hook to the jaw, Rodrigo was doing his own scheming. Waiting until they grappled briefly, the Mexican managed to hook a foot behind Ford's right leg to trip him up, and as he hit ground, kicked him in the head.

For a bad moment Gabriel couldn't see, couldn't hear the mob yelling to him to get up. But instinct drove him to spin his body and so avoid the vicious kick that missed his jaw by a whisker

His vision cleared in an instant and he was back on his feet, trading punches. Rodrigo retaliated with elbows and knees but Ford twisted and shifted his weight expertly to draw the impact from the other man's blows.

Suddenly full strength came rushing back. He feigned a semi-collapse when caught a glancing blow on the jaw. The Mexican dropped his guard in his eagerness to finish him off. As he rushed in, swinging, Ford measured him off and threw a bombing right cross that landed flush to the jaw.

Rodrigo was down!

Only now did the mob reveal whose side they were really on. They were yelling for Ford to finish his man off as it was plain the downed man was wide open for a king-hit to the jaw – and yet the finisher didn't come.

For good reason.

An inner voice reminded Gabriel that this was Carmelita's brother. He might not be too well-versed in good manners or polite behaviour but didn't need to be to know that beating up the brother of a woman you might be desperate to impress was hardly the smart way to go in this or any other town he knew of.

He suddenly stepped back and allowed his

arms to hang at his sides. Somehow Vega came erect. He wanted to keep on fighting even though he could barely stand.

'Call it quits, you dumb bastard!' Gabriel said roughly, even though deeply impressed. 'You're all through, so just back off while you can still walk.'

Stung by his words, Rodrigo threw a weak, wild swing that missed by a foot. His momentum carried him past his adversary who stuck out his foot to trip him up. He fell face down and by the time he was able to rise to one knee again, Gabriel was gone. Later the onlookers agreed that if they'd ever seen death in a man's eyes, it was in Rodrigo Vega's as he struggled into the saddle and rode away, raking cruelly with his spurs.

CHAPTER 5

MEXICAN GIRL

'Does that hurt, Mr Gabriel?'
'Only like hell.'
'Oh, then I'll stop.'
'I forgot to tell you I'm as tough as old

boot-heels. Keep going, Kitty.'

The hotel maid dipped her swab into the brine and once again applied it to Gabriel's broad back. Stripped to the waist he was perched on the edge of his hotel bed while the girl treated the vicious whip weals across his back and the right shoulder.

'You've sure got an awful lot of muscles, Mr Ford.'

'Broad in the back and weak in the head, as the saying goes, Kitty.'

'Is it true what they say? That you took Rodrigo Vega's whip from him then gave him the father of a hiding with it?'

'Maybe you'd best just tend my back and not ask so many questions, girl.'

'You're tetchy, aren't you? I suppose you know everyone says you're real tetchy?'

'Tetchy but tender,' he grinned. 'That's another old saying I just made up.'

'Oh but you do make me laugh, Mr Ford,' she giggled.

Gabriel sighed. Kitty was fat, forty and frolicsome. But she did possess a skilled pair of hands, while he was already feeling the benefits from the brine. He wondered how Vega was shaping right now. One thing was for certain. He wouldn't be out dancing the *cucaracha*.

'Up here,' he grunted, indicating the welt on his shoulder above the bandaging which she had placed over the deep cut from the whip.

Suddenly his eyes snapped wide as he turned his head. Looking confused but very lovely, Carmelita Vega stood framed in the doorway!

He came erect so swiftly Kitty almost tumbled to the floor. Ignoring the girl's curses, Gabriel stood bare-chested staring at the figure in the doorway, aching to go take her into his arms yet not certain he should.

So much had befallen them both since they'd last been together, and with him it had been all bad and bitter.

'Am I intruding?'

'Hell, no.' He smiled. Kitty was just patching me up but she was just leaving. Weren't you, Kitty?'

'I'm going,' Kitty muttered, gathering up her things. She looked Carmelita up and down as she went out with a sniff. 'I'd like to see how you'd get along relying on *her* to patch up your cuts and bruises, I'm sure.'

Gabriel grinned but Carmelita was grave as she moved deeper into the room.

'I was told you'd been injured, Ford,' she said. She was lovely in a form-fitting black dress and mantilla – very elegant, very Spanish. His heart ached to see just how beautiful she really was.

'Scratches,' he said.

'I heard all about the fight.'

'It was nothing important.'

'Rodrigo has taken to his bed with a bottle of brandy.'

'Good thing. Where's your father?'

'Visting Zebulon Moneros, probably to discuss you.'

'So ... that's why you were able to escape?'

'Yes.' Her eyes scanned his face as she drew closer. It seemed an incredibly long time since they had been alone together. They were almost awkward in each other's company, and yet Carmelita's dark eyes were glowing now and Gabriel felt a powerful surge of emotion and a pleasant tightness in his chest as he followed her every move.

'I-I missed you, Carmelita,' he finally got out.

'And I you ... my crazy wild *hombre*.'

And suddenly the ice was broken. With a sudden relieved laugh Gabriel swept her into his arms. Her head tilted back and she offered her mouth to his – lips as red as blood.

His embrace was fierce yet his kiss was tender, almost reverent. There had been endless nights in Sharrastone when he'd lain awake wondering if Carmelita Vega had been just a dream, some figment of a hard-living horsebreaker's imagination. But she was real as moonlight. And was now in his arms and murmuring his name over and over in a way nobody had ever done before.

This was the moment when Ford Gabriel realized it wasn't vengeance which had drawn him back to Coronado on the Rio. It was something far stronger.

Antonio Vega was an older and stouter version of his son. His dark hair was thinning a little but moustache and goatee beard were healthy and immaculately well-trimmed. Father and son shared a common arrogance and vanity. Both were widely admired and respected by the wealthy Mexican elite of Coronado but were viewed as hard, grasping and totally ruthless by others outside that small and powerful circle.

Vega senior was equally proud of his reputation with both these opposing classes. He welcomed the respect of his peers while viewing the animus of his inferiors as affirmation of his strength and status.

He had nothing but contempt for people

without property or power, doubly so should they happen to be gringos.

Vega stared at the imposing figure standing before him. He'd always regarded Don Zebulon as too carnal, violent and coarse-mannered to be classified as a genuine Spanish gentleman, even if the man's blood lines were impeccable and his wealth far in excess of Vega's own.

But at this vitally important time of his life, Vega found himself fully prepared to overlook his visitor's many shortcomings in order to concentrate on his attributes.

There was good reason for this change of attitude, for the imminent marriage between Don Zebulon Morenos and Vega's only daughter would unite the two most wealthy and powerful families along the great river and ensure that the blood lines would continue.

That consideration alone was more than enoughtto cause Vega to turn a blind eye to Morenos's weaknesses and many excesses.

Even before the proposed nuptials the two families had almost completed negotiations with the army to draw up a contract which would see all future beef supplies supplied by their two properties. That deal would effectively squeeze out a number of small

American ranchers who had supplied the fort in the past. With no other large beef markets in the region those small outfits would all go to the wall in time to be bought up eventually by Vega for next to nothing.

It would be tough on the American ranchers. But it was every man for himself along the Rio Grande. The Americans themselves had taught the Mexicans that lesson well in the past.

Now it was their turn.

Yet hitches could always arise to threaten even the best laid plans. It was in order to discuss one such obstacle that Antonio had arrived to visit with his prospective son-in-law that evening. The hitch in question had a name. Ford Gabriel, late of Sharrastone Prison.

'A mosquito,' Moneros said loftily when Vega broached the topic first. He mimed the act of swatting a mosquito against his neck. 'One does not waste time with a mosquito, Antonio, but squashes it without even thinking. No?'

Vega shifted uneasily in his hand-carved chair. Moneros worried him when he talked that way. The rich suitor for his daughter's hand had enjoyed so much power for so long that it seemed sometimes to Vega that

74

he regarded himself as above the law as it applied to ordinary mortals.

Of course the fact that Morenos had Sheriff Champion securely in his hip pocket only encouraged him to go too far on occasion. Vega was usually the more restrained and conservative even though there might be many a skeleton lurking in his wealthy cupboard as well. He was willing to bend the law when it suited but was rarely prepared to go as far as Don Zebulon.

'Gabriel's release and return must have come as a great shock?' Morenos remarked.

'I rarely allow scum to shock me.'

'A sensible man would surely not have returned to Coronado?'

'He is not a sensible man.'

'But he is a dangerous one. Are you aware he thrashed Rodrigo today?'

'Your son was reckless to confront him alone.'

'Rodrigo is proud.'

'Pride does not win battles. Power does.'

As he spoke Morenos jerked his head in the direction of the squat, powerful figure seated upon a leather couch in a far corner of this vast room. The pistolero named Chantaro stroked his luxurious black moustaches and stared back at the rich men with small diamond-hard eyes.

Vega frowned. In his joint campaign with his guest to force smaller ranchers from their land, he and Moneros had often been obliged to employ force, yet murder was not part of Antonio Vega's great plan for expansion and consolidation.

The man in the far corner was a killer.

He said, 'I don't want blood on my hands, Zebulon. But, having said that, Gabriel must go. Already there has been illicit contact between the man and Carmelita and I shall not permit that to continue.'

A change came over Moneros at mention of the girl. His face appeared suddenly heavier and darker, his eyes took on a hungry look. Moneros well knew Antonio Vega craved greater power and status yet these were things Moneros had known all his life. His passion now was for other things, and one of his greater cravings was his lust for the don's doe-eyed Carmelita, which was to be soon legitimized and validated through the holy sacrament of matrimony.

Had there been another way to get what he wanted he would have taken it. But there wasn't. Both father and daughter had made that perfectly plain.

'So,' he said, with just a hint of menace in

his voice now, 'what do you intend doing about Gabriel?'

'That is why I came here tonight, to discuss the matter, calmly and constructively.'

'Kill him.'

Colour drained from the older man's face. 'No ... no. Apart from the moral considerations there would be the risk.'

'Risk? What risk? I would merely slip Sheriff Champion enough gold and he would smooth everything over ... in the event of that horsebreaker's fatal accident. What could be simpler?'

Vega was finding his shocked pose difficult to maintain. For when his righteousness was stripped away, he could be as ruthless as a dog wolf himself. Linking the Vega and Moneros clans through marriage would elevate his family to a far higher level of wealth and social standing. He found it intolerable to think all this could be threatened simply because some lawman had secured the pardon and release of a roughneck horsebreaker, for no better reason that that he happened to be innocent.

He took a deep breath and forced himself to he calm.

'Surely...' he began uncertainly, 'Marshal McTigue might think it very strange should anything befall Gabriel so soon after his release from a prison sentence which is now officially seen as a miscarriage of justice. Rail-roaded into jail ... then killed as soon as he is released? Wouldn't you be suspicious in McTigue's boots? Damnit, man, we could end up on the gallows.'

'Have another drink. You are nervous.'

'Nervous perhaps. But also prudent, Zebulon.'

Moneros shrugged.

'So, you have heard my suggestion. What is yours?'

'I-I suppose I must come up with something...'

Moneros suddenly began striding up and down, his fleshy face set in hard planes and angles. He dumped his goblet on a table with an air of finality and hooked his thumbs beneath the lapels of his fine brocaded jacket.

'Don't take too long making a decision,' he stated in a hectoring tone. 'For I grow weary of the continuing delays to our plans for my betrothal to your daughter. In truth, I grow very weary. So much so I could be forced to look ... elsewhere for a bride.'

He paused to allow that to sink in, then went on.

'You may be surprised, Don Antonio, how

many patrons of fine Mexican families come to my door beseeching me to take an interest in their nubile daughters. Some of these daughters are very beautiful, and very rich. One never knows...'

Vega was certain the man was bluffing for he well understood his passion for his daughter. Even so, he was badly shaken. If the planned marriage failed to take place, then it was more than likely the proposed business merger between the families might also go by the board.

He could envision his lofty ambitions brought to nothing – all because of one swaggering gringo without a hundred dollars to his name.

'Leave it to me, Zebulon,' he said, collecting his flat-brimmed hat and making for the door 'There is a solution to every problem. The ceremony shall take place almost immediately. *Buenas noches* to you for now. Chantaro?'

The bodyguard rose to let him out. When he was gone the broad-shouldered gunman crossed the loom to Moneros's side as he was splashing liquor into a crystal glass.

'I think I know the solution to Don Antonio's problem, *patrón.*'

Moneros slugged his liquor down. 'What?'

79

'I think he needs a piece of lumber three inches wide and three feet in length.'

Morenos frowned impatiently. 'What the devil for, man?'

Chantaro smiled coldly. 'To strap to his backbone. It needs stiffening.'

CHAPTER 6

BIG NIGHT AT THE RIO SALOON

Following supper at the diner, Gabriel sat alone on a bench beneath the cottonwood to smoke a good cigar.

Little black bats did zigzags in the deepening sky as the first stars winked out. It was the hour when men sat out front on their stoops in shirtsleeves while their womenfolk paraded up and down in peasant dresses and low cut blouses.

The American girls were bolder and in many cases prettier than their Mexican counterparts, he observed. Yet the Mexican girls still attracted more. They had musical voices and lazy movements. They seemed to be made of softer stuff than the northern girls. They chatted with one another in lilting voices and glanced over their shoulders flirtatiously at the men strolling by.

As it grew dark and the sky swallowed the hills across the big river, three men rode by, Sheriff Champion and Deputies Dean and Tracey. They were heading off to the old Mex Town section where the sounds of a brawl could be dimly heard. All three glared across at Gabriel as they went by.

Gabriel gave the trio a big phoney smile to show he wasn't intimidated. Tracey spoke to Dean as they rode on. The lawmen were itching to come down on him, Ford knew. To them he was simply a troublesome ex-con and they knew it would improve their standing with certain influential citizens of the town if they were able to get rid of him.

The smile faded and his jaw muscles worked. Most likely the corrupt lawdogs would have to stand in line to have a piece of him, he mused. He was certain there were others in Coronado who would want to get to him first.

Leaning back lazily against the tree he drew deeply on his cheroot and crossed one boot over the other, a picture of relaxation. Yet he knew he was inviting trouble. He'd whipped Rodrigo Vega and had got to visit with Carmelita again. By now it was a fair guess that both power clans would like to see him at the bottom of the Rio with an anvil chained to his feet.

He was aware that during his stretch on the inside both the Vegas and Moneros had improved their wealth and power to a degree where maybe even the law itself might well be their servants and no longer their master.

Somebody here had planted a stolen horse on him a year back; that was something he'd never forget. He wasn't anticipating another stunt like that, maybe, but it seemed sure-for-certain his enemies here would never accept his return lying down. He knew he must keep eternally alert – just as he'd learned to do so efficiently behind the high walls of Sharrastone...

A man came off the walk and crossed to the bench. It was Jack Sibley and he'd brought along a bottle. They cracked it immediately and sat passing it from one to the other for a time before Sibley dropped the small talk and turned serious.

'Ford, I got a proposition.'

'No dice.'

'What? You don't even know what it is yet.'

'You're right, I don't. But I'm a hell of a guesser. Do you want me to guess what's on your mind right now, *amigo?*'

'Go ahead. I'll bet you a bottle you ain't even close.'

'Well, I say it's something to do with the so-called Ranchers' Association you're bossing. Right?'

Sibley blinked. 'Well, yeah, but–'

'The purpose of the association,' Ford overrode the man, 'is to fight anybody trying to take your beef contracts away and force you off your dirt. The "anybodys" are the Vegas and the Moneros clans. Is that what you want to talk about?'

The man looked puzzled. 'How the hell did you–?'

Gabriel winked.

'Jack, I've been keeping my eyes and ears open. You are getting kicked around plenty and some of your pards have already been beat up on and forced to sell out. You can't go to the law on account they side with the rich ... so then you get the bright notion that what you really need is somebody dumb enough and tough enough to help you just hold on to what you've got left. Me.'

Sibley's jaw hung open. 'Goddamn you to hell, man ... now I owe you a bottle. But how did you figure?'

Gabriel's expression turned sober. It hadn't

been difficult, he reflected. In prison he'd had inmates sucking up to him after he showed he could handle the biggest and worst of the Sharrastone heavyweights. He'd told them all to go to hell. Without a moment's hesitation he told Sibley the same thing now.

'But blast it, Ford, you're our only hope.'

'Then that means you got no hope.'

'I thought you cared about the little guy?'

Ford slapped his chest. 'I do. This little guy.'

Sibley was persistent.

'You need us as bad as we need you.' He gestured. 'Everybody is tipping you ain't going to last in Coronado with all the enemies you've got. But they are the same enemies we've got – the Vegas, Moneros and the law. All three. Cain't you see? It's a natural thing for us all to team together and stand up against them. More than that, we're prepared to pay you for helping us handle fellers like Chantaro and Rodrigo. We'd pay you good.'

Gabriel thrust the bottle away and stood.

'Where were you good old boys when I was being railroaded into Sharrastone?'

'Heck, we scarce knew you then.'

'And didn't want to know – then. Now it's different and you think you need me. Well, Ford Gabriel don't need anybody.'

'By glory! You really are the mule man, ain't you boy?'

'I'm my own man is what!'

He made to leave but Sibley jumped up and seized him by the arm.

'OK, OK, man ... mebbe I understand. But I gotta warn you about something. Folks know you're romancing that snooty gal, but maybe what you don't know is that the rich Mexes know about it too and are planning to fix your wagon. And I mean fix! A month ago a pard got his throat cut up-river. His crime was holding out on selling a piece of land to Moneros. We know Vega and Moneros were behind it but can't prove it. I don't want to find you floating face-down in the Rio Grande one morning, which I figure sure could happen if you keep playing what you're playing, and doing it alone.'

'I'm too cussed to die,' Gabriel said toughly. Then he eased off a touch. 'But thanks for the tip, Jack. Now you take one from me. You small men can't stand against these Mexes with money. So sell up and stay alive. Give 'em what they want and go start off afresh some place else. Just about any place would be better than Coronado.'

'You won't quit!' Sibley flared.

Gabriel gave a faint smile as he moved

away. 'That's because I'm a mule man.'

'You sure as hell are,' Sibley muttered dragging off his hat and scratching his balding dome. 'If you wasn't that way you'd join up with us for your own protection if for nothing else.'

But Ford Gabriel was already out of earshot, striding off along the street like a man who owned it. He had another date with Carmelita Vega.

The marshal's gun barrel made violent contact with Dan Hannigan's skull. Hannigan grunted yet didn't go down. Instead he reached for the peace officer with an animal growl emitting from the tangle of wild whiskers covering two-thirds of his ugly face.

'McTigue no good. Hannigan squash McTigue. Squeeze him.' Hannigan was a man of limited vocabulary but always managed to get his meaning across.

'The hell you will!' the lawman retorted – and laid a blow across the giant's skull that might have felled a mule.

It felled Dan Hannigan.

The junior marshals had brought the wild one in to be questioned about a minor theft. The prisoner had flattened two of them before switching his attention to flinty

McTigue. That was a bad mistake. Now he had a busted head and would draw jail-time for assaulting officers of the law

'They never learn,' McTigue sighed after they'd dragged the hairy one out. He was weary from a long day in the saddle but still mustered the energy to check out the mail which had accumulated on his desk during his absence. He frowned at a letter bearing a Coronado postmark, ripped it open.

'What is it, sir?' asked a junior.

'Just a response from Judge Osgood to an inquiry I made concerning that Gabriel fellow. As suspected he turned up in Coronado.'

'Seems to me you're still pretty interested in that hardcase, Marshal?'

McTigue passed a weary hand across his eyes. 'I'm more interested in whoever it was who framed him into prison. I surely do hate it when someone breaks the law and gets away with it.'

'Well, just between you and me, sir, I reckon you've already got your suspicions about who was behind that caper.'

'Suspicions don't add up to convictions,' McTigue muttered as he scowled at the letter. 'It's possible if Gabriel keeps on butting his head against the wall down there he could get himself killed. Then I guess I'd have something concrete to investigate.'

The younger man appeared shocked. 'You're not expecting this to happen, are you, Marshal McTigue?'

'Son, what do you think the cemeteries are full of these days?'

'Er ... might that be hardheads, sir?'

'Damn right.'

'You know, if I didn't know you better, Marshal, I might reckon you're a pessimist. That Gabriel feller is'

'Is none of your business ... or mine!' McTigue cut him off. 'Get busy!'

'Yes, sir!'

Gabriel and Carmelita strolled through the cedar grove which stretched from the high bluffs almost down to the Vega compound above the town. It was that time of evening when frogs began to croak and old Mexican women drew their shawls across their mouths to keep out the evil spirits they believed were abroad this time of night.

There was wild honeysuckle and the scent of sage in the night with a gentle wind coming out of Mexico stirring heavy boughs above their heads. The couple walked arm in arm, the man's dark head bent attentively to her words, her upturned face like a cameo in the starlight.

They halted at the edge of the trees. Carmelita stretching her arms before her and breathing deeply of evening fragrances. From the house came the sounds of a spinet. There was the whicker of a horse from the corral.

'You'd best go in.'

'I don't wish to.'

'You've likely been missed by this. Could be they have servants out searching for you already?'

'Are you trying to get rid of me, Señor Gabriel?' she pouted.

'No. Just trying to save you some trouble, is all.'

Carmelita sobered as she stared down at the house lights. 'Last night Father told me he's set the wedding date almost immediately. This time he will not be put off, Ford. I must do as he orders or—'

'Or what?'

'That I do not know,' she murmured, turning to him. 'Fly away with you, perhaps?'

'Maybe you shouldn't joke about things like that, Carmelita.'

'Am I joking? I am not sure.' Her hands linked around his neck. 'Tell me, what is to become of us, *hombre?*'

'Guess that depends.'

'On what?' she asked.

'Maybe on how you really feel about me,' Ford told her.

'You don't know?'

'You've never told me,' Ford replied.

'Nor have you told me,' she countered.

Gabriel was silent for a time. He realized she was right. He had never revealed his true feelings for he was unsure exactly what they were. Of course he knew he loved her, but beyond that lay a hundred uncertainties. A vast social gap separated them and he could never envision it closing. They stood worlds apart. He supposed he'd just been prepared for their situation to continue indefinitely without resolution.

So many uncertainties. Yet one thing he knew for sure, and realized it was time he made it known.

'I'm in love with you,' he said simply

Her eyes came brilliantly alive. 'Oh, *hombre*, how long I have waited to hear you say those words.' She kissed him fiercely. 'And of course I love you, and I always have.'

'You have?' He was stunned. Of course he knew she cared for him but hadn't dared hope it could be more than that.

They clung together in the starry gloom of the big trees for – who knew how long? It was exciting and wonderful yet the loner was already aware of nagging concerns and doubts.

'Carmelita, what you've just said is wonderful yet it seems to me it doesn't lead us any place.'

'What do you mean?'

'I've nothing to offer.'

'You love me. That is enough.'

'You can't live on love. You've always been used to everything in life. Nobody can go from everything to ... well, nothing.'

'If I had you I would have everything.'

He was almost relieved when he glanced away and sighted Antonio Vega pacing along the portico of the hacienda and glancing impatiently at his watch. He wanted time to think of what had developed between them. Maybe he wanted a shot of rye right now, even a couple of shots.

But ... she loved him.

That was an enormous thing to consider, doubly so when she was wealthy, privileged and educated while he was simply a working man who was very lucky not to be in prison.

He found his voice. 'I'll see you tomorrow, Carmelita. I'll be on the main street at noon if you can make it.'

'Goodbye for now, my lover.'

One last kiss and she was gone. She ran

lightly, like a young girl. Leaning the point of a shoulder against a tree with his face in deep shadows, Gabriel watched her go in through the scrolled iron gates and along the flagged walk to the lighted portico.

He saw Vega gesticulate angrily when his daughter appeared, then lift his head to stare around suspiciously as though searching for sign of somebody else, probably himself.

After several minutes father and daughter went inside and closed the heavy oaken door behind them.

Gabriel stroked his jaw as he turned to walk away slowly through the trees towards the river. He felt both elated and alarmed. Should Vega suspect anything serious between them he knew the man would not tolerate it. He would take steps, maybe send her away, possibly attempt to get rid of him as the source of the trouble? The one thing he could be sure of was that the second richest man in Coronado would feel honour bound to do something!

What if they should send her away? He brooded on this when he halted on a high bluff to watch the the river gliding by below. They might even pack her off to college in Mexico City until she 'came to her senses'. Then again, they might simply attempt to rush the marriage to Moneros through; rich Mexican families traditionally exercised the right to select their daughters' spouses.

Could he stop them taking such actions? That was one hell of a question to ponder on any starry night along the banks of the Rio Grande.

'Tuesday the sixteenth,' Antonio Vega declared, tapping the framed Dominican calendar with an unlit cigar. 'That is the day we shall announce your betrothal. You will be married at the church of San Angelo three days from that date, the nineteenth!'

Seated in the lamplit parlour with her mother and brother, Carmelita appeared composed even though far from it.

She had returned home to discover Rodrigo had had a posse of servants and employees out combing Coronado for hours, searching for her. She had been sighted in the company of Ford Gabriel despite parental warnings never to see the man again.

Her father had finally run out of all patience and insisted upon an immediate end to this foolishness and disobedience, once and for all. Within a week she would be the securely and respectably wed bride of the most eligible bachelor along the Rio

Grande. She was assured she could consider herself extremely lucky that the family had not had Gabriel arrested and shipped back to Sharrastone, 'From where he obviously should never have been released in the first place,' as her father insisted.

'And so, *señora*,' Antonio said smugly to his plump wife, 'you shall commence making the arrangements for the gown, the feasts and all the guests in order to ensure this shall be remembered as the greatest occasion in Coronado's long history—'

'Father!'

'Yes, daughter?'

'I shall never wed Zebulon Moneros!'

A stunned silence engulfed the great room. It was one thing to flirt with an undesirable suitor, another entirely to defy one's parents on such an all-important issue as matrimony. Although the family knew the girl had never been enthusiastic about the older Moneros, no high-born Mexican lady ever told her family she 'would not'. Obedience here was the paramount virtue.

'You shall indeed marry him,' Rodrigo declared, when he'd recovered from the shock. 'Blood of the Saviour! Such insolence. You are pledged to marry him and you shall.'

'I shall not!'

Her father, Antonio, brought his fist crashing down upon a table. His face was livid. 'Why do you say you will not marry the man who loves you?'

Tears brimmed in Carmelita's eyes. 'Because I love another man!' she cried, and fled from the room.

A shocked silence engulfed the room. The don and his lady stared at one another, Antonio plainly horrified but the donna less so. The clock ticked loudly as Rodrigo slowly rose. He moved across to the sideboard where his bullwhip lay coiled. His fingers caressed the smooth plaited leather as he spoke with his back to the room.

'Gabriel!' His voice and face were like iron.

The don raised his goateed chin. 'Go do what must be done.'

Rodrigo scooped up the whip and left the room without looking back.

'Another, Gabriel?' grunted the barkeep.

'Yeah ... give me another.'

The shot was poured and Ford turned with the glass in hand to lean his muscular back against the edge of the bar.

There were fewer than a dozen customers in the Rio Saloon, yet because it was small, the room appeared crowded. Although the bar was down at heel it was still a good place to do some serious drinking – and thinking.

The piano rattled discordantly while the fat Mexican accordionist delivered a sad old song all about unrequited love.

Gabriel slugged half his shot and felt the warmth of the spirits hit his belly. His eye was drawn by Jack Sibley's brooding group of ranchers in a far corner, yet he didn't really see any of them. His thoughts were far from the Rio Saloon, at the big house upon the cedar bluffs.

The rear door opened and three men entered. They were Americans employed as herders by the Vega clan's cattle interests. As Ford glanced up the batwings bellied inwards to admit a bunch of Mexicans and Americans. Each was a Vega rider and all wore a look of common intent as they closed in on the solitary figure at the bar.

They didn't have to make any announcement for Gabriel to know he was their target.

For a moment or two he felt tempted to draw his .45, yet decided against it. Outnumbered five-to-one, he might well go down should gunplay erupt. Yet scarcely had that thought registered when the brawny leader of the bunch suddenly rushed at him with a curse, hauling his right fist back to throw a mighty swing, leaving him no option.

That punch never connected.

Gabriel snatched up a heavy chair and brought it down on the attacker's skull with enough force to fell a steer.

This hardcase was no steer. He went down like a typhoid victim and Gabriel side-stepped a second man then kicked his legs from beneath him to see him come down with a rafter-rattling crash.

Moving even swifter now, Gabriel drove a shoulder into a bloated belly with sickening force and lined up the ashen-faced attacker for a kick that might have put him in plaster, had it landed. It didn't. Someone had slipped around behind Gabriel and his first aware-ness of this was when something smashed across the back of his head. Glass sprayed over his shoulders as he reeled against the rickety bar.

He'd been slugged with a bottle.

He managed to land one roundhouse right flush in a contorted face before finding him-self going down beneath a mass of humanity, being borne aloft and toted swiftly for the rear door.

Now he wished he'd taken a chance and used his six-gun instead of losing it.

He thought he heard Jack Sibley shout his

name as the outside air hit him, but couldn't be sure.

The cold night air revived him a little. He drove an elbow venomously into a man's eye and kicked another where it hurt the most. But they had him and he knew it. He was hauled roughly across to a hitching post and lashed to it with rope. As he tried to head-butt a man with a face like a toad, he glimpsed them parting to make way for the tall and elegant figure under a black sombrero. Something in Rodrigo Vega's hands glistened like a snake in the starlight.

'There is only one kind of reasoning your breed understands vermin!' Vega hissed. And struck.

The whip sliced through Gabriel's shirt leaving behind a crimson weal across his back. The pain threatened to lift the top of his head yet at the same time cleared his brain – fast!

He twisted away from another blow from the whip and brutally head-butted another man holding him before absorbing another cut from the whip.

Both strokes hurt yet magnified both his anger and strength. Fighting the ropes with everything he possessed, he felt them give and increased his furious pressure.

A snarling figure rushed in to tighten his bonds only to be felled by a flying missile from behind as several Americans burst through the doors.

The man crashed across a prone Gabriel who tasted blood in his mouth as he struck the floor and rolled against legs, then heard the shout:

'Into 'em, boysl Give 'em Larry Dooley!'

Gabriel managed to kick his way under falling bodies to get his back to a wall and, still seated, watched admiringly as Jack Sibley led his drinking pards in a headlong attack against the Vega men.

It was pretty to watch until suddenly watching simply wasn't enough.

He jumped to his feet, cupped both fists together then swung them like a mallet to catch a brawler to the side of the head and drive him clear through a window which shattered in a shimmering shiver of glass.

Snarling furiously, the man from Sharrastone lowered head and shoulders and went at Vega like a runaway wagon.

The rich man was smashed on to his back and remained there as Gabriel deliberately hauled back his right foot and delivered a kick to the short ribs that would surely have slowed down a buffalo.

It slowed down Vega – totally – and Ford was swinging his attention to the main ruckus when a bull voice shouted that the law was closing in. The law here was no friend to Ford Gabriel or his rescuers. By the time Champion, Dean and Tracey had ridden into the rear yard of the Rio Saloon, the only brawlers left were Vega men – and most were down upon the littered floor.

'Sorriest looking bunch I ever saw,' the law remarked later, and he did not exaggerate.

CHAPTER 7

SHOT DEAD

It was cheap whiskey he was drinking but Gabriel could not recall enjoying a stiff shot more. He held his glass out for a refill, then carefully raised it above his shoulder and allowed the contents to spill out slowly over his shoulders through the hole in his ripped shirt.

He grimaced when the sting came. But it was a relieving pain which quickly faded, as the whip scars themselves would fade:

given time.

He drank the next shot at a gulp.

Someone handed him a fresh shirt which he drew on then leaned back gingerly against the outer wall of his hotel room. He took out his cigars. The tin case had been dented in the ruckus but the contents were undamaged.

Ranchers, cowhands and a bunch of American day labourers were either sitting or standing about, relaxing. Sibley was in charge of the liquor, while a bowlegged little rancher moved about briskly with strapping and liniment, still patching up those who'd been in the thick of it.

Scarce anybody had escaped either a bruise or black eye. Despite this an air of goodwill prevailed. They'd rallied impressively after Sibley raised the alarm, and despite bruises and busted noses they knew they'd scored a win over the enemy comprising all the manpower the two biggest rancheros were able to muster.

As he got his fresh cigar going, rancher Venn Buell showed up to report that the lawmen had already returned to the jailhouse. A husky young man around Gabriel's size and age, Buell said that as far as he knew Champion did not intend taking further action over the big dust-up, which they interpreted as good news – for them.

Ford got his cigar going to his liking and nodded to Buell. 'Did you get to take a look around the Vega compound?'

'Yeah, done like you asked, Ford. I seen the medico leaving a spell back, so I figure that means he didn't have too much serious patching-up there either.'

'Any sign of Carmelita?'

'Sorry.'

She'll be all right,' Sibley assured. 'Mexicans don't rough up their womenfolks, not the aristocrats, leastwise.'

'No,' Gabriel said soberly. 'They just force them to marry somebody they hate.' News was already out concerning the marriage.

'That sure ain't right,' Sibley agreed. 'But what can you do?'

'I'll think of something,' Ford said quietly. His features relaxed a little as he gazed around. 'Don't think I'm not grateful for the way you boys weighed in there today. I surely am. Surprised, too. Guess I didn't figure anybody gave much of a damn about anybody else in this man's town until you showed–'

'Elope,' Sibley broke in.

Everybody stared.

'What?' Gabriel queried.

The rancher's leathery face became animated. 'Run off with Carmelita Vega and that solves your problems. And when there ain't any wedding to join her folks and the Moneros clan together, it will surely knock their plans to form one big Mex combine into a cocked hat.' He chuckled. 'Hell, sometimes my ideas are so bright I scare myself.'

If Ford was impressed he kept it well hidden. 'You're loco,' he growled. 'You talk like you got knocked on the head in that ruckus.'

'Never clearer in the thinking department,' Sibley disagreed. 'Look, you are sweet on that little girl and don't want to see her throwing herself away on Moneros. If she loves you like you say she does she'd jump at the chance to run off with you, boy. Hell, it'd be – romantic!'

'I can tell you what isn't romantic,' Gabriel countered. 'And that is living rough when you've been used to living plush – like she'd be lining up for.'

Several heads nodded. Buell's was not one. 'If you ask me, that purty woman ain't all that interested in plush living and fancy trimmin's. If she was she'd have snapped up Moneros long ago.

'It's still loco as I see it,' Gabriel insisted,

though not as forcibly as before.

Sibley shot him a sly look. 'Of course, if you've no objection to her winding up in the fat arms of a greasy bastard who feels so scared and guilty that he's always got to have a killer for a bodyguard, then that's an end to the argument, *amigo.*'

A quietness fell. Every eye was upon Gabriel as he moved along the balcony, sipping his whiskey and scowling like a man with a king-size headache. He could see right through every man jack of them, he told himself. They were as transparent as pure brook water. They just wanted to see him run away with Carmelita in the hope it might foul up the merger.

Then an inner voice reminded him he would not be doing it for them, but for Carmelita...

An ugly image invaded his mind. He was seeing Carmelita and Moneros embracing – naked. He'd never let his thoughts dwell on that ugly possibility before. Yet if he didn't act fast, how could it help become a reality?

It was unthinkable. It was like a slave market. The Vegas had no right to sell their daughter off to the highest bidder. But the reality was it could happen unless somebody intervened. Maybe somebody about six-one tall with a tetchy temper and a jailhouse background?

Now – who did he know fitted that bill?

'You've gone mighty quiet and thoughtful,' Sibley remarked at last.

'It's still loco!' he said for the third time. Yet there was no conviction in his tone now. And when his jaw muscles began working they could all sense his mind was already grappling with the challenge of how it might be done.

'Loco but right, man,' Sibley urged quietly.

'A man could get killed.'

'Somehow I've always had the notion you're just plain too ornery to kill...'

Moneros sat in the back room of the bordello with a bottle.

He was a regular visitor. They knew his wants and catered to them, for a price. Satiated and half drunk, he sprawled in a plush velvet chair and watched the woman dress.

She was a healthy, comely girl, several shades lighter than the swarthy Moneros. The tint of her skin was almost golden and it went well with brown eyes and heavy dark hair. As she bent to draw on her satin slippers her deep breasts lolled against the peasant blouse. When she glanced up to see his eyes upon her she smiled professionally. Even so, she was unable to conceal a hint of distaste.

Moneros suspected all the whores hated him because he was rich and vicious, but mostly because he was rich. Everyone envied him for his wealth he believed – no other reason made sense.

'Get out!' he said. 'It wasn't worth two pesos, let alone twenty.'

The girl shrugged and left. Don Moneros wasn't the only customer, merely the wealthiest.

He drained his glass and had jerked the bell cord for another drink when the madame came in to inform him that Chantaro had arrived and was waiting in the yard. Moneros drew on his waistcoat and hat and quit the perfumed room, going quickly down the rear steps to the yard where dark horsemen waited in the starlight.

The powerful figure of Chantaro strode forward from deep shadow and threw a salute.

'Well?' Moneros growled.

He had handpicked the men who'd been busy on his behalf throughout that afternoon and evening.

Their task had been to probe every corner of the big river town to investigate persistent rumours that something big was in the wind in the wake of the clash between the Vegas people and the Cattleman's Association. Moneros was disgusted by the Vegas's ineffectual attempt to deal with Gabriel. Don Antonio had warned him of both Carmelita's astonishing confession and her affection towards Gabriel, and Moneros had raged ever since.

He reckoned even a horsewhipping mightn't deter that horse-wrangler. Moneros was now resolved to take full command of the worsening situation but his first step before making a move would be to give him a clear picture of what exactly was taking place.

He'd have had Chantaro plug Gabriel and toss his carcass into the Rio but for Marshal McTigue's puzzling interest in that troublemaker. With that ringy lawman involved, a man simply couldn't afford to make a slip-up, even if his name was Moneros.

This was his cautious side making its presence felt. Yet standing there in the starlight with a ring of silent, hard-faced horsemen surrounding him reassuringly, Moneros knew if it came to a straight choice between playing it safe or losing Carmelita he would forget about playing safe.

He nodded silently and Chantaro made his report.

'There is surely something afoot, *patrón*. There has been much activity amongst the small ranchers in town throughout the day – much coming and going. And a spy at the Vega house reports that Carmelita received a smuggled note this afternoon which caused her great excitement. And last – but possibly most important of all – Gabriel told the desk clerk at the Rio Grande Hotel that he will be checking out tonight.'

'Leaving? Moneros sounded relieved. 'Do you believe he has finally had enough?'

Chantaro's uncovered head shook slowly. 'Not that one, Don Zebulon. On your instructions I have watched this *hombre* closely. He walks the streets with a boastful swagger and has been seen in protracted discussions with Sibley and others.' He tapped the side of his fleshy nose with a forefinger. 'Something surely cooks, *patrón*, and it is more than old fish.'

'Well, do not make me guess, man, Moneros said irritably. 'What do you think is afoot?'

'I know not. But there is surely something I ... feel it in my bones.'

'Then what do you propose?' Moneros

was not too proud to defer to his protector at such times.

'We must simply continue to maintain a continuous watch on everybody as before, Don Zebulon, and be ready and prepared to act the moment we sight anything suspicious.'

'Act?'

Chantaro's face grew darker in the half light. The man breathed heavily through flared nostrils, like an animal.

'I mean kill, *patrón!* If there is a plot afoot tonight then we can be certain that its success would come at great cost to the Vegas, or even you. Our enemies have grown confident because of Gabriel. We can not permit them one more victory. Next time, we must be ready to strike!' He emphasized the word by slamming a fist into his palm.

'Do whatever must be done,' Moneros said with sudden decisiveness. 'But do it swiftly and secretly. Just remember McTigue.'

Chantaro smiled like a wolf. 'Of course, *patrón*, even marshals can die...'

'On your way. I return to the hacienda to await the news.'

Within half a minute all horsemen were gone from the yard leaving behind a faint patina of dust hanging in the night sky.

From a high window, two worn-out women looked down.

'Now what do you suppose that was all about, Gladys?'

'Could be they was all making plans to attend Holy Mass in the morning?'

They laughed at the irony and went back to work. It was busy at the bordello and other places as well, that night.

All was in readiness.

Their saddle horses were concealed in the cedar woods a quarter-mile from the great house, and the men of the Cattleman's Association had supplied a pack horse laden with supplies. Gabriel figured if they could make it across the Rio Grande without the alarm being raised they would be so well lost in Old Mexico come first light that there'd be no catching them.

Yet the most uncertain part of the operation still lay ahead. Carmelita must first escape her parents' house.

Gabriel and Venn Buell watched the Vega place from the trees. It was almost eleven o'clock, the scheduled time. Ford had not seen Carmelita since the previous night, but had proposed their elopement by note, and had his proposal accepted. By return note.

He envisioned a day some time in the future when he and Carmelita might sit by a fire reminiscing on the romance, excitement and uncertainty of this night, providing nothing should go wrong.

'I see something moving, Ford,' Buell hissed. The young cattleman had volunteered to help them escape while other ranchers and supporters were in town creating an impression of innocent, boisterous relaxation.

Watching intently Gabriel kept fingering his hair back off his forehead, an unconscious sign of tension. He'd had an uneasy feeling ever since they had taken up their positions here. He had an edgy feeling somebody was watching them, or that something unexpected was about to happen. But that was it, he kept telling himself. Crazy. There was no sound reason for believing it all wouldn't go off like clockwork.

Ford narrowed his eyes to pick out the slender figure crossing the shadowy courtyard. There could be no doubt it was Carmelita. He felt his heart skip one full beat. He knew just how much hung upon the next minutes ... the next seconds even.

Now the wall cut Carmelita off from sight. The two men stared intently at the courtyard door, waiting for it to swing open. It didn't. They exchanged taut glances when they heard the faint rattling sound and saw the solid door shake.

'It's locked!' Gabriel guessed. 'They must have locked up in case she tried to get out to meet me again.'

'Look!' the other said suddenly, pointing. 'She's climbin' over!'

Gabriel held his breath when he saw the slender figure swing nimbly astride the wall. At that moment the house door giving upon the courtyard opened and a slab of light fell across the yard. Carmelita released her grip and dropped to their side of the wall and disappeared in the flanking brush.

The figure of Rodrigo Vega stood in the lighted doorway; staring out at the night. After a long moment he vanished inside and the door banged shut behind him. The two watchers waited anxiously for sign of the girl, until they sighted a pale arm waving from the wall shadows.

'She must have hurt herself when she dropped,' Gabriel panted. 'I'm going down there.'

'No! You go get the horses while I go tote her out of the grounds. But if she's hurt you'll need to have the horses ready by the gate. In that case, we'll just have to take our chances on being sighted.'

Ford didn't like it, but there was nothing he could do about it.

'On my way.' he panted. 'You're a good man, Buell.'

Buell just grunted and broke away from the tree-line in a low crouch to go snaking down the slope towards the compound. Everything now seemed reassuringly quiet as he reached the tall, scrolled-iron outer gates which gave onto the rear of the Vega headquarters.

Opening the gates he slipped stealthily down the stone-flagged pathway to the courtyard wall, where he found the girl crouching in the shadows.

'Ford? Oh, it's Mr Buell. I twisted my ankle.'

Just relax, *señorita*,' he whispered. 'I'll get you out. Ford is just fetching the horses.'

He lifted her with ease, came erect, glanced sharply left and right, then hurried back for the gates. Once there, he set her down gently so that she might stand, clinging to the gates for support. Then he stepped through the gates to look towards the treeline for sign of Gabriel.

He never heard the shot that killed him.

It came from a clump of hackberries on the

far side of the natural clearing from where he and Gabriel had watched the house. The bullet went clean through his heart. He fell with a surprised look on his face, feeling as if a horse had kicked him in the chest. The final sighing sound to escape his lips was drowned out by the deep-throated reverberations of that single gunshot as he rolled onto his back, staring up at Carmelita with blind eyes.

The girl screamed in horror, the sound ripping through Gabriel like a knife as he came storming through the cedars astride the sorrel. Bursting into the clearing, he sighted the girl first and then the motionless figure at her feet.

'Over there, Ford!' she screamed. 'The shot came from there!'

Doors were flinging open in the mansion as Gabriel used hands and heels to send the sorrel pounding across that dangerous open space. But in those desperate seconds he wasn't thinking of anything but the hidden gunman. Had he attempted to rescue Carmelita they might well both have been killed.

His revolver was in his fist as he drove the horse headlong into the hackberry thicket, the muzzle sweeping this way and that, hunting for a target. Moments later his quick eye caught movement beyond dark trees.

114

He heeled in that direction, ducking beneath plucking limbs and thorny vines. In an instant he saw them spurring off along the yellow ribbon of town trail, two sombreroed horsemen riding hard.

Leaning low over the sorrel's neck, lips skinned back from his locked teeth, he raised the .45 to eye level.

Buell dead. An honest, hard-working young man who only wanted a good life. Stone dead at the Vegas's gates, leaving a wife and two children!

The .45 bellowed, its thunder carrying out across the town. Once, twice, three times he triggered. The trailing rider faltered, while Gabriel saw the lead man twisting in his saddle, the starlight glinting on the long barrel of the pistol in his fist. He recognized the powerful shape and flamboyantly expensive garb of Moneros's sinister bodyguard the second before the gunflash sent him ducking low.

The bullet missed ... barely.

The second shot, coming instantly upon the heels of the first, struck the sorrel squarely in the chest. Man and horse went down in a crazy swirl of roiling dust and flying hoofs. Gabriel kicked free from the rolling animal, his whole body jolting brutally as he slammed into a ditch.

He lay stunned, fighting desperately to clear his spinning head. To think. His first cogent thought was that he'd dropped his Colt. Next moment his brain snapped clear of the grey fog threatening to envelop it and he rolled and sprang instantly to his feet.

The sorrel lay dead in the middle of the trail. The saddle had burst loose in the crash and lay upside down in deep dust. His six-gun lay in clear sight yet was all of twenty feet distant. He'd started off towards the weapon before casting a glance down the steep, right-hand slope.

He propped.

There was a wounded man down there, bleeding and cussing. And heading back towards his downed henchman, Chantaro, riding recklessly fast.

Instantly the rider cut loose at him.

Gabriel's headlong dive into lank dead grass carried him close to his six-gun. A slug whammed into a rock close by and howled off into the sky in a whining ricochet. The next shot was wilder, enabling the desperate Gabriel to hurl himself forward, clap a hand over his gun – then use it!

There was next to no time to aim, yet luck or providence was with him. The bullet went close enough to a raging Chantaro to spoil his next shot, thus giving Ford time to dart back and go to his heavy saddle, which he hauled before him like a shield.

He shuddered as the enemy gun sent a two-ounce chunk of lead into the rig. The slug penetrated almost all the way through the under layer of padding and leather. Then it was Gabriel's turn – and the Mexican *pistolero* was without cover!

His first bullet creased Chantaro's arm and the second drilled a hole in his hat. In a split-second, the lethal gunman decided his henchman wasn't worth the risk, and demonstrating dazzling athleticism, hurled his body downhill, twisting and turning as he rolled while Gabriel's lead came howling after him until a bullet from another quarter caused the Texan to duck low.

Squinting through grass, he realized Chantaros's wounded pard was upon one elbow, shooting at him.

Two bullets whined many feet overhead.

He realized instantly the man was no real danger. Deliberately he lined him up in his sights. All he had to do was squeeze the trigger and there would be one hardcase less to make life dangerous around Coronado.

But dead Mexes told no tales, nor could

furnish any useful information.

The half-hidden figure fired again, this shot even wilder than the previous ones. Gabriel calmly took aim and squeezed his trigger to drive a bullet so close to the prone figure that he jumped a foot into the air and spilled his six-shooter.

'Just freeze or the next one will take off the top of your skull!'

Gabriel sounded like he meant every word. Maybe he did. Miguel the Mexican believed him anyway.

'*Por favor*, Gabriel, do not kill me. I am a Christian.'

'If Christ knew the kind of followers he has here,' Gabriel growled, getting up, 'he'd get back upon the Cross and start all over again.'

The man began to weep. Gabriel looked for sign of Chantaro. There was none. At the bottom of the slope the man had rolled down lay a fissure which he'd plainly used as an escape passage.

Nursing a deep flesh wound in his thigh and a bullet burn along his left forearm, the wounded man was weeping softly when he reached him.

He quivered as Gabriel hunkered down before him and rested his hot pistol muzzle against his temple.

'Who shot Buell, chili-eater?'

'Do not kill me, Gabriel. It was Chantaro!'

'Why?'

'We-we watch the *casa*. Chantaro suspects there is something afoot tonight, so while others watch the ranchers and the town, we watch the Vega house. We see someone sneak in and reach the wall after the *señorita* appears. We think ... we think it was you. So Chantaro shoots.'

Gabriel nodded grimly. He suspected he was hearing the truth. Buell had been gunned down in mistake for himself.

'Gabriel ... I bleed!'

'Who cares?'

Yet he pouched the Colt and applied a tourniquet to the thigh wound. There was a hell of a lot of blood about. Maybe it was the main artery. A man could die from that unless he got proper care fast.

He was considering his next move when he heard voices and looked up sharply to realize the Mexican was no longer his responsibility. People were arriving on the scene from the direction of the town, drawn to this blood-spattered stretch of trail in the wake of the gunfight. The wounded Mex would survive, he told himself as he got to his feet. Too bad Buell was past all help.

CHAPTER 8

IN ENEMY HANDS

'Carmelita!' Antonio Vega's voice had a razor edge. 'I said you were forbidden to come down here!'

'I simply had to see that Ford was all right,' the distraught girl insisted thrusting her way through the crowd cluttering up the trail. Relief flooded her pale face when she glimpsed Gabriel standing in a bunch speaking with rancher Jack Sibley. Ignoring her father's protests she ran across directly to seize him by the hand.

Ford slipped an arm around her shoulders, staring over her dark head at the Vegas. He saw Antonio speak to his son, who nodded and came striding quickly towards them.

'Carmelita, I am to return you immediately to the house,' Antonio stated.

'She'll go when and if she's ready, Vega,' Gabriel retorted. Coated in dust with his shirt ripped half off his body, he looked double-tough by the light of the rising moon. So much so that Rodrigo Vega hesitated, fingering a badly swollen mouth that was a legacy of their recent clash, suddenly unsure.

'Here's the sheriff!' someone shouted, and all heads turned to see Champion and his deputies ride up followed by Moneros and several of his riders, with Chantaro boldly riding drag.

'By God and by Judas!' Gabriel breathed, dropping hand to gun handle. He lunged away from the group and gesticulated to Champion. 'Sheriff, arrest Chantaro. It was him who murdered Venn Buell!'

Reining in sharply Champion put a questioning stare on Moneros as he ranged up alongside. The don looked every inch the feudal lord in that moment as his cold stare travelled from the wounded Miguel to Gabriel.

'Chantaro a murderer?' he exclaimed. How could this be when he has not once left my side all night?'

This brought a roar from the ranchers who'd already heard Gabriel's account of the killing, and believed it. Champion immediately hauled his six-shooter to pump a shot into the sky to quieten them down.

'That'll be enough of that!' he declared in a

hoarse voice. 'Don Antonio, is it correct that a man was shot and killed at your hacienda?'

'Regrettably, yes.' Vega appeared pale and drawn as though he might genuinely regret the killing. 'But I am not certain how it came about, Sheriff Champion.'

'Then I can sure as hell tell you,' Gabriel broke in forcefully. 'Buell was gunned down from cover by that gunshark son of a bitch yonder. The man didn't have a hope in Hades. I took off after Chantaro and his pards, and I winged the ugly one, Miguel.'

'Cold-blooded murder, then,' Sibley breathed. 'Champion, you got your duty to do. Arrest that man!'

'*Uno momento,*' Moneros said with authority. 'One moment. I doubt that we have heard the full story. Tell me, Gabriel, what were you and Buell doing skulking about the home of my friend Don Antonio in the dead of night?'

'What's that got to do with anything?' Gabriel countered.

'Perhaps everything.' Moneros jerked his chin at Chantaro who sat his saddle with one leg hooked over the horn and picking his teeth with a split match. 'I swear that this man against whom you wish to lay such grave charges was at my side as he is always supposed to he. But what about you, Gabriel? What were you doing up here?'

'Yeah,' Champion growled. 'What?'

Gabriel shot a look at Carmelita. The girl shrugged and spread her hands in resignation. 'You must speak the truth, Ford. It will emerge anyway.'

A grim Gabriel knew this was so, sucked a deep breath into his lungs, lifted his jaw. 'I'd come to take Carmelita away,' he stated. 'We were fixing to elope so she wouldn't have to marry a man she hates.'

The sheriff was tempted to touch off another shot to quell the excited hubbub that greeted this remarkable admission. Yet the mob eventually quietened of its own accord in order to catch whatever Antonio Vega was saying.

'Carmelita, my daughter, this cannot be true.' The rich man's face was pale with anger. 'Impossible!'

'It had better not be true,' Rodrigo said menacingly.

'Why, what'll you do, Rodrigo?' Gabriel challenged. 'Kill me? You mean you haven't seen enough death for one night?'

That struck home and Rodrigo immediately fell silent, shaking his head. It was plain to everybody that the Vegas, both father and son, were taking Buell's death much harder than was Moneros.

Don Moneros appeared to be regarding the fatal incident more as an inconvenience than a tragedy, and one that should be settled and put behind them as quickly as possible.

'Sheriff Champion,' he said arrogantly, 'I strongly suggest ... no, order, that you take this man into custody pending further investigation of this whole ugly affair. We have just heard the jailbird level the grave accusation of murder against my bodyguard, though not heard one word from him concerning a motive.'

He paused as though inviting comment. When none was forthcoming he cleared his throat and continued.

'Very well. Now we learn also that Gabriel himself was involved in the most offensive crime possible to any Mexican of breeding, namely, invading the sanctity of home and family. Might it not be possible, gentlemen that this Buell fellow may have been shot by someone who saw two men acting suspiciously out by the hacienda? Or could it simply have been a case of rogues falling out? We already know Gabriel has been involved in all the shooting out here tonight. Perhaps it was his bullet which pierced Buell's breast?'

'No!' Carmelita cried. 'I was there. I saw the shooting. It was not Ford.'

'Perhaps we need more than the hearsay of an overwrought girl,' Moneros said maliciously. 'Surely the testimony of a young female still obviously suffering from the shock of an attempted abduction is not to be taken too seriously?'

Both Gabriel and Carmelita began to protest, but Champion shouted them into silence. He would look deeper into the affair immediately he stated. The principals would immediately adjourn to the Vega hacienda and everyone else could go home and clear the streets. The principals, as he identified them, were the Vegas, Gabriel, Moneros and his bodyguards and his deputies.

'What about Miguel?' Gabriel demanded. 'He admitted to me that Chantaro killed Buell.'

'That man is wounded and plainly in need of urgent medical attention,' Moneros said smoothly. 'He is also quite feverish. I fear that anything Miguel told us now would be unreliable and of little value. Don't you agree, Sheriff?'

Champion agreed. A weak man, he would have agreed had Moneros insisted black was white by this stage. 'I reckon under the circumstances you'd better hand over your gun before we go to the house, Gabriel,' he said heavily. Deputy Tracey, collect that man's sidearm, will you?'

Deputy Tracey rode forward eagerly. He hadn't forgotten that Gabriel had made him appear a fool in the hill country.

'Let's have it, hardcase,' he said roughly. 'The likes of you shouldn't really be trusted with a sidearm, anyway, any time.'

It was a testing moment for Gabriel as he stared past Tracey at Moneros, Chantaro and the Vegas. He was aware of a powerful feeling of deja vu, of having lived through this before. It was like a re-enactment of the scene out at his horse camp in Dead Crow Canyon when everybody showed up to 'discover' a stolen horse amongst his cavvy – the plant that had resulted in his being sent to prison.

This in turn brought a jolting new thought. Was the whole murderous affair tonight just another setup? Another attempt to frame Ford Gabriel as he'd been framed before, and by the same people?

His stare drilled at Chantaro who was smirking behind his luxurious moustache. He was half-tempted to whip out his .45 and deal with that *pistolero* in the same way

Chantaro had done with poor Buell.

But, of course, he would not. He was no killer, nor would he risk doing anything that could jeopardize Carmelita's safety. As both Moneros and Champion doubtless well knew.

'C'mon, Gabriel, we don't have all night.'

The .45 seemed to weigh a ton as he hauled it from leather. Gabriel's bleak gaze flicked over Jack Sibley and his ranchers. They plainly expected him to fight. Yet they were simple men. They didn't realize this was a very different situation from the one at the Rio Saloon.

He didn't glance at the deputy as he handed him the Colt. He wasn't looking forward to the next hour.

The only sound in the big room for a time was the scratching of the quill pen as Sheriff Champion completed writing up the depositions he'd taken. The lawman was a slow penman as he was ponderous and deliberate in all other things.

Yet the only man irritated by the man's slow progress appeared to be Gabriel. The others had good reason to feel relaxed, for, cued by Moneros, they had so altered their versions of the killing that it was now beginning to appear that the guilty party had not been Chantaro – but Ford Gabriel.

The yard man reported to have heard the shot had rushed out to see Gabriel near the dead man with a gun in his hand.

The Moneros' *vaquero* claimed to have witnessed the entire affair while simply 'passing by', and claimed actually to have seen Gabriel cut Buell down.

Chantaro had assured the sheriff he had been in the company of his *patrón* all night long, due to the fact that Don Zebulon appeared to be afraid Gabriel might come after him, after having beaten up Rodrigo.

Gabriel sat alone in a corner, smoking. Carmelita had found him a shirt before being banished to her room, yet he still appeared dusty and dishevelled in the wake of the violence. Moneros and Antonio Vega had overruled his demands that Carmelita be permitted to give her version of the shooting, and Champion had let them get away with it. He'd even demanded they fetch Judge Osgood, but this had been rejected also.

His enemies' intentions were only too plain. They planned to railroad him right back into Sharrastone.

Or on to a gibbet?

He found it hard to believe that everything

had gone so wrong, so fast. Just two hours earlier he had been contemplating a new and exciting life with the woman he loved. Suddenly he was staring down a one-way street leading to hell.

But he was a long country mile away from throwing in his hand...

'You know,' he said, 'that there iron-mouthed marshal is going to be mighty interested to hear about all of this. What was his name again, now? Oh yeah, McTigue. Marshal McTigue...'

Champion ceased writing and Moneros stopped puffing on his cheroot. Antonio Vega suddenly appeared to be under a strain as he nervously toyed with his whiskers. His son, who'd said very little during the entire session, looked questioningly across at Don Moneros.

'I would not place too much hope in the marshal, horsebreaker,' Moneros said, unruffled. 'Anybody might reverse a rustling charge. But murder is a very different matter.'

'I didn't murder the man,' Ford snapped, coming to his feet. He slammed Champion's desk with a fist. 'They're lying, and anyone with half an eye could see it!'

The deputies started forwards from their

posts by the door, but Moneros waved them back.

'You are beginning to come apart, Gabriel,' he said with some relish. 'Well, I suppose we should not expect courage or dignity from any man who would stoop so low as to attempt to abduct an innocent girl from the bosom of her family.'

Champion rustled his documents.

'Uh-huh ... er, that abduction charge ain't going to help your chances in court none, I'm thinking, Gabriel.'

'You are going to look pretty stupid trying to prove that when it comes to court,' Ford warned. 'You might be able to stop Carmelita from speaking up here tonight but there is no way you can keep her from testifying in court. The judge will demand it. And when she confirms that we were eloping, and that she knows I didn't shoot Buell, McTigue will demand to know just what the hell you lying bastards are trying to prove.'

'I wouldn't count on Carmelita's appearance too heavily if I were you, convict,' Moneros said. 'If you know your law you would know a wife is not obliged to furnish evidence against her husband that may be damaging. If you were to make such allegations of collusion and perjury against me at

130

the trial, her testimony could damage me–'

'What are you mouthing about? You're not her husband!'

Moneros flicked a speck of cigar ash from the sleeve of his velvet jacket.

'No, I'm not. But I shall be by the time you are brought to trial.' He nodded to Antonio Vega. 'You see, I have decided in light of tonight's events, *compadre,* that Carmelita is at risk. This man has obviously confused and upset her – in fact I have decided that our marriage should take place almost immediately By doing so, your daughter shall pass under the mantle of my protection and so be safe from anything this vermin might try to do in the future. You agree, of course?'

Vega nodded like a suddenly old man. The events of the night had left him badly shaken. He did not believe Gabriel had shot Buell, but rather found it quite easy to accept Chantaro as the killer. In truth Vega was deeply sickened by it all. But it was too late for him to draw back now. If he failed to support Moneros there was every chance everything here would blow up in his face, his plans for the future and the security of the present ... everything he prized.

'*Uno momento!*' Rodrigo said suddenly,

getting up. 'I do not think this a good idea, *patrón.*'

'What must be done, must be done,' his father said.

'I believe my sister has been through enough,' Rodrigo continued stubbornly. 'To force her into a hasty marriage at this time could be very bad for her, I believe.'

Arguments broke out all over the room at that point and Ford Gabriel was a silent but intent listener as he eased across to a small side window to catch some air.

He had been kept under close watch ever since the arrival of Chantaro and his deputies, yet they had become increasingly distracted by the unexpected flare-up between the aristocrats.

Right at that moment a calm-looking Ford Gabriel was a desperate man. The horse-thieving affair had demonstrated graphically just how any innocent man might get railroaded in a rich man's Coronado. It still seemed a formal murder charge could not be made against him yet he couldn't be certain.

And with the shadow of a noose hanging over the eventual outcome, a man really needed to be certain...

His right hand lifted to touch the sill casually. Chantaro glanced his way but was diverted when Antonio insisted Moneros leave his son's discipline to him.

Slowly and imperceptibly Gabriel lowered himself into a crouch with knees half-flexed. He bunched powerful thigh muscles and sucked his lungs full of air while continuing to appear normal and casual.

Then exploded into action.

Coming up out of the crouch in one athletic lunge he sprang up at the window and used upraised arms and elbows as a battering ram to smash out window panes and braces in a shimmering shower of shattered glass.

His velocity carried him clear through. With glass fragments still showering down about him he plummeted six feet straight down to hit the courtyard pavement, kicked and rolled, bounded erect.

He was off in the instant, pelting across the court as angry faces filled the window behind. A shot thundered but the bullet went wild and smacked a tree.

He zigged and zagged like a dervish and seemed to be making for the main gate. That was a ploy. At the last moment he swerved violently to go pounding along the base of the wall at a speed that left bullets spanging harmlessly behind. He launched himself into a headlong dive that carried him through a little side gate which gave access to the outer court.

The court had a gate leading to a wide street.

He went through it like a shot.

He could dimly hear angry voices bawling for horses as he streaked along the down-sloping street. But he wasn't concerned. Not now. He had a good head start and reached the first of the clustered houses and twisted laneways which crowded along the base of Coronado's east hill with still no sign of pursuit.

Plunging into the first alley he came to, he promptly vanished.

Don Antonio Vega slumped in the jailhouse chair, looking like somebody who had been chased across the hills by a relay of hounds.

The don had ridden as vigorously as a man half his age in the pursuit of Gabriel but was now exhausted and feeling all his fifty-three years in his bones.

Champion was equally spent and glistened with oily sweat as he rummaged in a desk drawer for the inevitable flask. The sheriff still had his deputies out combing the streets along with Chantaro and men from the

Moneros and Vega outfits, but wasn't hopeful.

Voices sounded outside and Rodrigo and Don Moneros came in together.

Despite harbouring doubts concerning Gabriel's guilt, Rodrigo had nonetheless thrown everything into the manhunt. He had just returned from scouring the river banks both north and south of town but had only managed to nab one half-starved peon who'd swum across from Old Mexico with his mule searching for a new life in the land of plenty.

Moneros alone appeared fresh. The strong man never soiled his hands with menial tasks – that was what he employed others for. He had in fact spent the past half-hour at the Rio Grande Hotel sipping tequila while awaiting word on Gabriel's recapture.

That news was yet to come, which ensured the don's mood had switched to foul as he strode in now. He poked Sheriff Champion out of his own chair with his staff and took the lawman's place. He chose to sit brooding with all nervous eyes on him until he characteristically shrugged and emerged from his tantrum to throw the most positive light on the situation.

He chose now to take the view that even if Gabriel wasn't caught then at least the threat he'd posed was by this probably extinguished. He barely gave them time to digest this when continuing confidently to announce his intentions of bringing the wedding forward.

In a growing expansive mood, he went on to disclose he no longer held any reservations concerning recent violent events. He admitted freely that Chantaro had indeed gunned Buell down. But in self-defence of course, certainly no crime involved. His captive audience seemed to accept this readily enough. He proceeded to reveal how he'd delegated his men to shoot on sight if they spotted trouble, and when Chantaro had seen someone he mistook for Gabriel sneaking from the house with Carmelita he'd simply thought it his duty to bring him down.

So ran his story.

Only Rodrigo had the gumption to opine that Chantaro had no right to open fire even had it been Gabriel at the gates. His own father quickly silenced him, however.

The spirit appeared to have deserted Antonio Vega. He was a hard and ambitious man but not a ruthless one. He was appalled by recent events. He had fallen amongst killers. Yet he was too deeply involved with Moneros to withdraw now. It was like riding a roller coaster with no way of jumping off.

He saw no option but to place himself in the hands of Moneros who seemed never to lack either ideas or the energy to put them into practice.

Moneros insisted he'd simply tackled the Gabriel threat, head on. That events had blown up in their faces was plainly nobody's fault. Too bad Gabriel got away, but the prime concern now was to safeguard against any eventuality which might arise from this situation.

'If Gabriel is not caught,' he stated, 'then we must at least ensure that his teeth are drawn. How and why? Consider this. While my people can be relied upon to keep their mouths shut, and will, there is one danger as I see it. Carmelita!'

They stared in puzzlement. What was he driving at?

He told them – straight from the shoulder.

Although shocked at first by his proposal, eventually Rodrigo and Antonio gave in and so made approval unanimous amongst the great families of Coronado.

Rodrigo was last to fold, and as soon as he did Moneros sent him off to roust out the padre.

Moneros knew his law and was aware that

no Mexican wife could testify against her husband should that husband ever be un-lucky enough to find himself charged with murder.

CHAPTER 9

ONE MAN'S WAR

He was awakened by the chill in his feet. Tugging the Hudson Bay blanket off his face Gabriel blinked out at a brand new day and wondered just where in hell he was.

Then he remembered. The town, the gunplay and riders hunting for him all over before his decision to cut and run.

But that tactic only applied for what had remained of the night. Now, there was much unfinished business awaiting down there in the town a mile below and he had to tackle it while there was breath in his body and a woman on his mind.

He flung the blanket aside and rose to stretch his body. He stood with head tilted back facing the thin light of dawn breaking silently across the high country. Within mere moments it seemed the whole eastern horizon had come alive suddenly to shine as brightly as the honed blade of an Apache scalp knife.

He grinned at this piece of imagery, then nodded in sober satisfaction as he flexed his arms and stretched his lean body tall. The way he felt assured him he'd been smart in lying low a spell. He now felt ready for anything.

The light of the lamp daubed the judge's features with a ruddy glow and glinted from the monocle he'd set in his right eye in order to take a long steady look at the night caller.

'You know, Mr Gabriel, I've been rather expecting to meet you face to face again ever since I'd heard you were back among us.'

'As I recall, I didn't think much of our last meeting, Judge.'

'Nor did I, sir, nor did I. And for very good reason. For although vaguely dissatisfied with much of the evidence presented against you on that occasion, there was certainly enough of it that seemed solid to convince me the punishment was warranted when I packed you off to Sharrastone for a year. My underlying doubts concerning your guilt, as we both know now, were later substantiated.

And if you are wondering if all this adds up to an apology, young man, then it certainly does.'

They were cheering words to hear. Ford needed them. But there were other things he needed more this uncertain Rio Grande morning.

He nodded. 'I need your help, Judge Osgood.'

'Well, I didn't figure you'd knocked me up in the middle of the night to ask after my health.'

'You might as well know I'm in trouble.'

'Of course you are. They are claiming you murdered a man up at the Vega hacienda earlier tonight, then escaped from custody.'

'You heard it all then?'

'Most of it. You see, although I spend a great deal of my time these days locked away reading and writing in this room, Gabriel, my friends and contacts always manage to keep me abreast of whatever's happening in this town – my town, as I like to think of it.' He paused then gestured. 'Well, take a seat, man, take a seat.'

Gabriel sat down warily.

He genuinely believed the judge was straight, otherwise he wouldn't have risked coming here. Yet he could not afford to trust the man fully, nor virtually anybody else in Coronado tonight for that matter. He wanted to believe his .45 and natural fighting skills would continue to protect him now, yet the odds against him surely had to be shortening by the hour.

'Would you care for a shot?' Osgood reached for a large bottle. You certainly look like you could use one. You got scraped up taking a short cut out of the Vega house, so I'm told?'

Ford nodded and leaned back, beginning genuinely to relax some now. He found Osgood's bluff and honest manner reassuring. 'And yeah, I could sure use a drink.' He'd had a couple with the cattlemen but was still edgy. The town appeared to be crawling with armed men hunting him today and he could scarce claim to be surprised about that.

Osgood hummed to himself as he splashed brandy into snifter glasses. The man responsible for a judicial district which stretched one hundred miles along the Rio Grande was a well-read and independent-minded old jurist and scholar who'd ridden a racehorse all the way from New York to Texas in '44 to escape city life and never ventured back East again.

'There you go, young Gabriel,' the man

said, handing him his glass. 'Good luck.'

'Reckon I need all of that I can get right now.'

Osgood occupied his desk chair. He was dressed in crumpled black pants and a frill-fronted shirt liberally splotched with egg. It was said the judge always ordered three eggs whenever he dined out, two for himself and one for his shirt.

No snappy dresser this, but he was a fine justice, reliable and honest. This was no small thing in a town where the sheriff took graft publicly on the main stem like a bull buffalo licking up salt, and wealthy Mexicans acted as though they truly believed the law had been designed for their own private convenience and profit to manipulate anyway they chose.

The judge took a slug and didn't pull his punches. 'Well, did you kill Buell?

Ford wasn't surprised by his bluntness. He'd expected it. That was Osgood's way.

'No.'

Osgood picked up a pencil and adjusted his monocle. 'Then tell me who did. Maybe you'd better tell me everything while you're at it.'

Ford nodded, impressed. He wanted the judge at least to know the full truth in the event he didn't survive whatever lay ahead of him. Specifically, he needed Osgood to understand exactly what had transpired up on the hill, then seek the man's advice on what his next move should be.

So he kept talking. By the time the judge had jotted the whole story down in his fat journal it was time for another slug of fine Maryland brandy.

'Chantaro,' Osgood murmured reflectively, swirling the liquor around his glass. 'That man is a born killer. You mightn't know it but he slit a rancher's throat here less than a month ago. I knew he was guilty as well as I know my own name, but that's as far as it went. He'll never stand trial for that killing and it's highly doubtful he'll be called upon to answer for murdering Buell either. He's too well protected by his master and all his minions.'

'Are you admitting Moneros can still get away with whatever he likes here Judge?'

'Virtually, I fear. Just look at the reality of his situation. The man has money, prestige, an old family name steeped in Rio history, plus a whole mess of folks who would do just about anything he wants of them rather than risk his wrath. I despise Don Moneros but will readily concede he has far too much

143

power and influence for either me or the office I represent.'

'So ... are you telling me you can't help me?'

'To my shame, that is so.' The judge leaned forwards, expression intense. 'But though what I have to say to you now must shock you to your bootstraps, and although the gods of jurisprudence will hate me for it – I'll say this to your face, straight and plain. You don't really need a judge, Gabriel.'

'What?'

The older man leaned forward, weathered features alive and intent.

'I have tried every which way I know to clean out the vice, patronage, vote-rigging and rampant corruption in this town, only to learn bitterly and at great cost that this cannot be achieved under prevailing circumstances. What you really need to help you get some results and maybe – let's hope for everybody, myself included – clean out the corruption of power here ... is a mean-mouthed, hard-bitten two-gun US marshal!'

Ford blinked at the older man before the nickel dropped.

'You're talking about Marshal McTigue, aren't you, Judge?'

The judge slapped both knees.

'Got it in one. Look, wire him urgent over in Rumtown, son, that's my best advice. If anybody can help you, he can. Better still, why don't you go see him? It's too easy to turn a man down in a letter or a wire.'

'I can't leave Coronado.'

'Why not?'

Gabriel came to his feet.

'It might sound loco, but I'd be too scared to go. I guess I'm scared what could happen here while I was away.'

'You're thinking of that girl. Right?'

'Correct.'

Osgood rose and let the monocle hang down his shirt front. 'Well, I suppose if I was maybe two hundred years younger and a girl like that was interested in me, I would likely feel the same as you do.'

He sighed resignedly, snapped his braces.

'Well, I'm sorry I can't be of more help, son. But should your case ever come to court I'll represent you personal and fight tooth and nail to get to the truth and clear your name, even if I couldn't guarantee results. A stack of false-swearing witnesses can reduce any court to a farce or get any man hanged in this benighted county – as I know to my everlasting shame.'

'Thanks anyway, Judge.' They shook

145

hands. 'But I'll fire that wire off to McTigue and just hope he might show up here before I or anybody else gets killed.'

'I wish you well, Gabriel.'

It took Ford time to make his stealthy roundabout way via the back streets in order to reach the unpainted telegraph office, where he roused out the operator and fired off his urgent wire off to Rumtown. Evading several foot-weary searchers with rifles still out hunting for him, he was keeping low while attempting to re-establish contact with Jack Sibley when he bumped into the rancher quite by chance in a back alley behind the Pair of Dice Saloon.

Turned out this wasn't such a coincidence as he might have thought, as he realized when Sibley revealed he'd just spent the past two hours in a town-wide hunt for him.

How come?

He quickly discovered Jack had some intriguing and puzzling information to relate. A short time ago one of his sidekicks had witnessed something strange taking place over on Bluff Street in the shape of a pair of Hacienda Rancho hands seemingly 'escorting' the padre for Cedar Hill.

'The padre?' Gabriel puzzled. He rested hands on hips as he turned to stare off at the

146

Vegas' gleaming white compound which crowned the crest of the river bluffs. 'What do you suppose might be going on, Jack?'

'Well, mostly when folks send for a preacher somebody is either dying – or getting married.'

'Getting married?'

Carmelita Vega examined her hands with an air of total concentration. She turned her palms upwards, studied them for a time, then slowly nodded her dark head. It was reassuring to know that some things were still the same, that there were still realities like your own solid flesh to prove some normality still existed in a world which seemed to be turning completely crazy.

She needed whatever reality she could find on a night when her whole life had been tipped upside down and her future irrevocably changed.

It was still difficult to believe so much could happen in so short a time!

In the space of just a few short hours Carmelita had firstly made the momentous decision to elope with the man she loved – then witnessed a man murdered in cold blood and an innocent man accused of the killing.

It was as though in a relatively short space of time her entire orderly existence had been turned upside down to a point where she feared she could soon hear herself agree white was black.

'Will you please stand up straight so I can see if the dress is the right length, *señorita?*' the weary maid sighed. The woman was attempting to get Donna Vega's old wedding gown to fit her daughter's trim figure. Even if the maid also believed the world had gone crazy, she plainly did not care, providing this all-important garment was completed in time.

'What does it matter if it's right or wrong, Marie?'

Carmelita's tone was lifeless and the tears were starting again as the door swung inwards and her brother entered the room without knocking.

Rodrigo Vega appeared strained and pale with a whip coiled over one shoulder. Wordlessly he held the door open and jerked an imperious thumb at the servant girl. She left immediately. He kicked the door closed and moved deeper into the room, staring at his sister in her fine white gown.

'The padre's here,' he stated flatly. 'He's still half asleep. But he's here and ready to do as he's told, so I suppose that is all that counts...'

'Then – then it's not all just a hideous nightmare, Rodrigo?'

'No, it's all too real.'

'I'm grateful that you ... tried to stop it. I'll always love you for that, my dearest brother. And for all the other things you have done for me.'

The young man stared at her like somebody struggling to accept and believe something with all his strength, yet without success. In that moment Rodrigo Vega was trying to convince himself even at this eleventh hour, that he was dreaming, yet knew deep down it was all only too real – just as real and tragic as his sister's bitter tears.

The wedding would take place. His father had said this and his word was law.

Rodrigo had a strange look in his eyes as he absently stroked the smooth surface of the whip he held and cocked an ear to the sounds emanating from other parts of the great house.

Brother and sister had always been close despite sharp differences in character. So strong and protective in fact was their relationship that Rodrigo had actually risked challenging his father on Carmelita's behalf concerning what Vega was causing to happen here tonight.

Inevitably the challenge had failed and that should have been an end to it. But the proud son knew that whatever the other outcomes of this grotesque day, the ever-widening rift between father and children would never be healed. Not now. In the space of a single day the Vega siblings had finally seen their parent stripped naked and exposed for what he truly was. A man without grace, obsessed only with power and status – gross, grasping and possibly even murderous.

And if that was not enough, now young Rodrigo was being commanded to stand by and witness them marry his beloved only sister off to a man she did not love simply because that union would fulfil his father's ambitions and satisfy another man's lust.

'It's … it's simply infamous, Carmelita,' he said in a strained voice. 'We have always been taught that the *patrón* of the family is to be obeyed as one would obey God … but this thing goes far beyond all that. It is wrong. To force a marriage in such a way surely is sacrilege. Don Moneros claims it must be so in order that as his wife you would be unable to testify against him in court – somewhere in the future. That is rubbish. It's really you he wants ... and he has seized upon this excuse to claim you. I would rather see you in the house of a penniless gringo peasant than united with such a one. At least Gabriel is a man!'

'Please, Rodrigo, you are only making it worse. There is nothing to be done but to go through with it now. I grow weary of defying Father. I – I just can't do it any longer. And neither can you, my brother.'

There was nothing entirely new in this situation. For brother and sister this was always the way it had been, being reared under the strict patriarchal Spanish system as it applied to the family The word of the father was law – and yet young Rodrigo Vega's every instinct chafed against that law now. He'd tried yet failed to curb the anger and resentment his father and Moneros had unleashed in him simply by insisting upon this grotesque parody of a Christian marriage.

He was tonight a man torn between tradition and love for his sister as they quit the room together for that flower-scented stroll through the lamplit courtyards for the family chapel.

The strains of the Mexican Wedding March, played softly on an organ, swelled in

151

the night.

The distant sounds of music rippled over the stealthy figure snaking across the Vega compound beneath a row of flowering azaleas – less than fifteen feet from the closest sentry post.

Other men with guns were positioned throughout the walled garden courts which flanked the great house on both the northern and eastern sides of the compound. Coloured lamps filled shadowy recesses and alcoves with brightness while the music rising from the floral circle somewhere up ahead convinced Gabriel he had guessed right in figuring where the ceremony would take place.

The rose garden grotto had been his best guess. It stood secure behind high walls and was beautifully laid out as he remembered from several stealthy trysts shared there with Carmelita almost under her parents very noses.

And standing in the centre of grotto, the family chapel!

It was a soft cool night with a three-quarter moon climbing the eastern sky, and he remembered hoping, back in the past, that one day he might get to marry the woman he loved in this beautiful setting.

How could he ever have been such a fool?

'Keep your mind on what you're doing, damnit!' warned the back of his mind. 'No noise, keep low, make it to the grotto … then play it from there…'

A trickle of cold sweat snaked down the back of his neck as he crouched within the leafy folds of a giant rhododendron bush. He waited patiently, not breathing, while a shadowy figure with a gun passed on by in soft-soled shoes.

He was at first disgusted to realize he was actually nervous. Yet on consideration he figured it was not fear for himself that grabbed him. For he knew he was ready to risk his life, if needs be. But never hers.

What if what he was attempting should result in the girl he loved losing her life?

That was an ugly thought to a man from out of no place. Yet he'd banished it within an instant with an iron act of will – a trick of mental discipline conceived and learned the hard way in the breathless silences of those coal-black nights down in Sharrastone's hole where a man had no way of knowing if he would ever again see daylight or hear again the voice of another human being … should they choose to leave you there to rot.

He inhaled deeply and was rock calm as he took fresh stock of the situation.

Both the Vegas' hands and men from Hacienda Rancho were here in force ... as expected. For nothing must be allowed to interfere with their plans, or more correctly the plans of Antonio Vega and groomsman Don Moneros. Doubtless his enemies might figure him insane enough to try something tonight; there could be little doubt that every sentry he'd sighted while infiltrating his way into the enemy heartland was out hunting him.

During that past hour which had seen him steal his way past a number of armed sentries at last to gain these lush gardens of the inner compound's southern side, he'd willed himself to believe Lady Luck was his saddle pard tonight. Yet simple common sense now warned that this capricious Lady could dump a man in the blink of an eye without a second thought.

He'd be loco to ignore reality.

Don Moneros had long been the strong man of Coronado, he realized. And this night would provide him with a showcase to demonstrate just how much absolute power he really did possess. Here, everybody from the law and church through to the entire

Vega and Moneros clans and a guest list of powerful ranchers and dignitaries, were being granted an intimidating vision of what the future would be like once the great families were united.

That starkly simple vision was clear. With himself at the head of the historic union of families, Don Zebulon Moneros would be truly and finally *numero uno* – and whatever *numero uno* wanted – he would take.

That was a life lesson Ford Gabriel had learned once before and might well die attempting to challenge before this night was over.

Sweat stung his eyes as he compacted his body into a dark corner in the flung shadows of an ornate stone fountain in one of the outer courts, as the sounds raised by another two sentinels drew closer.

His eyes dropped to the Colt .45 in his fist as he forced himself to make one last appraisal of the odds. And thought: one against so many?

They would slaughter him!

He reined in that sickening lurch of doubt and was strong once again. Solid. And thought: remember your mission, hardcase! Fail and Carmelita will be legally wed to a man she fears and despises. You've got just one direction to travel. Straight ahead for the chapel – there's no way hack. Not now!

He raised his head sharply. The sudden surge of organ music warned that the time to act was now. Now!

More sentries passed from the flower-bedecked court. He waited for them to disappear then streaked for the rose garden grotto in a low darting crouch.

A short time later found him snaking through the beautiful circular garden of the grotto proper. He raised his head to peer over, expecting to sight the bridal party only to sight more men with guns!

No bridal party preacher or even an organ. He realized only then that the music he'd been hearing was emanating not from the garden itself but someplace beyond. The chapel?

He slid down to the ground and his heart began to trot. He knew exactly where the family chapel stood in the shadow of the great house's west wing, and cocking his head, confirmed the music was coming from that direction.

He froze.

More armed figures passed by his hide. The moment they were gone he legged it across open moonlit space to gain the shadow of the mansion's thick adobe southern wall.

Where a burly man with a rifle stood with boots spread apart facing the chapel ... while the organ music was beginning to grow stronger.

With action now the only option he went up and over the six-foot gate with the agility of a racoon, dropped soundlessly to the ground and lunged forwards.

The sentry heard the soft stutter of boots. He whirled and flung up his rifle. Gabriel's elbow smashed into his face. A knee to the guts doubled the guard over and a savage chop to the neck finished him off. Ford supported the slumping figure but couldn't prevent the rifle dropping with a clatter.

'José?'

The voice came from the smaller gate giving onto the inner court. Gabriel sprang forwards as it began to open. A bulky Mexican clutching a weapon thrust his head around the gate and Gabriel wrapped a six-gun barrel around his skull. The man's legs shot from beneath him and he went down like a well bucket.

Two giant bounds and he was finally within the inner court with his .45 at the ready.

The area lay momentarily empty before him!

He permitted himself a grunt of relief then darted across to the chapel's east portico where he propped, frozen in the wash of light spilling from the window.

The music had stopped...

CHAPTER 10

YOU DON'T OWN CORONADO!

Soft lamplight gleamed on the padre's balding dome as he stood by the little altar merely pretending to pray while struggling to prepare himself for a duty he would rather avoid, and would if he only had the courage.

For although Coronado's portly priest loved God, he feared the rich and powerful of the temporal world far more. And Don Moneros, the man whose marriage he was to preside over here tonight, was the one he feared most of all.

The organ murmured from the vestibule as the padre turned to watch the bride as she began the slow walk down the aisle upon her father's arm. For a moment the breath caught in his throat. He thought she looked at once both the most beautiful and most unhappy young woman he'd ever seen.

As though in total sympathy with the bride-to-be, her father looked as though he'd needed several stiff shots to prepare him for this ceremony, while in her pew, the mother sniffed and dabbed at eyes which she kept downcast.

In sharp contrast the best man wore a revolver only partially hidden under his coat and smelt of cigars and gun oil. The bride's brother stood at the rear of the chapel with an expression more suited to a funeral than a family marriage ceremony.

Don Zebulon Moneros saw and sensed all this tension and uncertainty, and simply didn't give a damn.

In truth it seemed that only the bridegroom himself appeared to be enjoying it all. Impressive in a fine black velvet suit with starched white shirt and string tie, the don smiled and bowed to his bride-to-be as she joined him, then turned to nod imperiously to the good padre indicating he should begin.

Obediently, for he was a Moneros man as much as was the weakling sheriff who stood watching from the foyer, the padre opened his leather-bound missal and began to read.

'Brothers and sisters, we have gathered

here today in sight of our Divine Lord to celebrate the joining together of–'

He stopped abruptly as a sharp curse drifted in from the arched doorway. Sheriff Champion was the offender, and when everybody turned in his direction they realized the lawman was now entering the chapel proper – walking backwards!

For a moment nobody understood. But no longer than that. Next instant, a suddenly pale Don Moneros choked out a curse upon sighting the face directly behind Champion's shoulder. It was Ford Gabriel and he held a big black revolver at the lawman's temple.

'Ford!'

The disbelieving cry came from the bride-to-be as she whirled away from the altar to go rushing back down the aisle. But her father Don Antonio proved swifter and sprang forward to seize her with one powerful hand while fumbling for his sneak gun with the other.

Gabriel's shout rang through the chapel like a gunshot. 'Don't try it, Vega! I swear I'll cut you down if you force my hand!'

He was bluffing but nobody knew it. And staring into the muzzle of that naked gun even the arrogant Vega faltered, and his daughter felt his grip slacken. 'This … is not possible!' the man choked, all colour gone from his face. 'Nobody could get past our security ... you should be dead...'

'Take another look. It's me and I'm here!'

With those words Gabriel prodded Champion ahead of him down an aisle flanked on either side by frozen faces. The .45 in his fist flicked directly at the gunman, Chantaro. 'One move from anyone and you'll die first, killer!' he warned, and all could see the deadly gunman believed him when he froze. Then he raised his voice. 'Now I am leaving here – with Carmelita. Release her, Vega!'

Then Gabriel thrust a shaking Champion down into a pew seat. Still nobody moved. To a man they appeared frozen by that big black-muzzled gun and the fierce face behind it.

'I know I can't whip everybody you've got outside, but I'll sure kill a bunch if anyone dares try and stop me.' Holding an entire room under a single gun, Gabriel was gambling and knew it. Yet he appeared somehow both invincible and lethal as he locked stares with Don Antonio Vega – and was. For this ex-con, this was an all-or-nothing roll of the dice.

'And speaking of shooting people ... if I was half the scum you painted me ... you'd

161

be number one on my list, rich man. I reckon any father willing to sell his own daughter to someone twice her age with the reputation of a dog sets a new level in low, even for you, Vega–'

Movement caught the corner of his eye and he brought the Colt muzzle whipping around to freeze upon Chantaro as the gunman's hand stole towards gun butt.

'I said I don't want to hurt anybody but I'd make an exception in your case, too – killer. Give me half an excuse and you'll die now – instead of some time ahead when the law works it out you murdered Buell.'

'You can't prove that, Gabriel!'

'Judge Osgood seemed to think different when I gave him the whole story. And you'd better know I wired Marshal McTigue who's already on his way. Now, Carmelita and I are leaving – and I mean now!'

It was a big bluff which he almost pulled off. Almost...

The padre stifled a gasp when from the altar position he glimpsed Don Zebulon's left hand slide behind his cummerbund to produce a small two-shot pistol while nodding almost imperceptibly to Chantaro and allowing the gunman to see the weapon in his hand.

Chantaro's response was immediate. 'Tracey, Dean!' he bawled. 'We'll all take him down – now!'

The gunman was bluffing. He didn't dare make a play with Gabriel so close. In any case, Tracey and Dean remained too frozen by fear to move as Ford suddenly went lunging down the aisle to drag Carmelita free from her father – and only then did Chantaro's swift hands blur towards Colt handles.

Chantaro now reckoned he could draw and shoot before Gabriel could trigger. He was almost proven right, for Ford was a brawler, not a gunslinger. Yet he was also desperate enough to achieve a capability in a crisis which would normally be impossible.

The bellow of Gabriel's Colt rocked the chapel like a bomb to end a split second before Chantaro's sixgun reached firing level.

Ford triggered again and the bullet tore through the stricken gunman's throat.

Chantaro jerked trigger but his bullet slammed into the floor as he reeled backwards, clawing at his bloodied neck with his weapon clattering harmlessly to the floor, eyes already glazing. Ford's bullet had smashed through his spinal cord and it was a dead man who toppled over the low altar-rail to fall at the fat padre's feet.

Pivoting, his head ringing from the gun-blasts, Ford plunged for the exit clutching Carmelita's hand only to face the reality of the two-shot that had filled Moneros's other hand. He braced himself for the fatal bullet – which didn't come. Instead there was a double blast of gunfire from the far side of the chapel which caused Don Moneros to jerk violently and slew sideways as Rodrigo Vega's shots smashed into his ribcage.

Gabriel watched Moneros fall with crimson staining his fine black jacket, badly hurt yet still clutching his gun; then he swung violently about as Deputies Dean and Tracey came rushing into the chapel.

'Get Gabriel!' the yellow sheriff shrieked, diving for the safety of the floor.

'No!' Rodrigo shouted. 'No more shoot–'

His words were drowned by the vicious spang of Don Zebulon's sneak gun. Ford gasped as the slug creased his back. Instinctively, he twisted and fired in the one motion.

Zebulon was attempting to work the two-shot a second time when the bullet hammered into his chest and sent him tumbling backwards upon the altar with a bullet lodged in the heart.

Chaos!

Gabriel dived low again as gunfire thundered in this place of worship where the air was already thick with gunsmoke. He quickly realized no bullets were coming his way but were instead lancing to and fro between a gutsy Rodrigo Vega and the two deputies who were lawmen in name only. Dean immediately collapsed to his knees, coughing blood. But the wiry Tracey lived up to his nickname of Hotshot as he blasted from the hip to send Rodrigo Vega reeling back against the wall, his face a sudden ash grey.

Barely taking time to aim, Ford let fly at Tracey to catch him in the shoulder It was not a serious wound but did expose a coward who'd simply been lucky with the guns until that moment. Howling like a dog and discarding his gun the man dived for the doors to disappear into the night leaving blood splotches in his wake.

Champion was bellowing orders at Dean until cut off in mid sentence when a charging Gabriel reached him from behind to bring the butt of his Colt down upon his skull. As the man's face slammed into the bloodied carpet, Antonio Vega, ignoring his wound, charged the wounded Dean and backhanded him twice across the face before ripping the smoking .45 from the dead man's fingers.

It was a bad moment for Gabriel when he twisted to see Don Antonio facing him across the tumult of the chapel with gun in hand.

But this wasn't the arrogant don they all knew. This was a man who had needed the grisly sight of dead men and his own son leaking blood to strip the blinkers of arrogance from his eyes and see just where greed and ambition had led him. In that moment of revelation he was finally remembering what a real father was supposed to be.

The unfired gun clunked to the floor and the don's ragged shout filled the building.

'It's all over!'

He lurched to a bullet-shattered window and leaned out, gesticulating wildly. 'It's finished, and I, Don Antonio, decree it. Every man, throw down your weapons. There'll be no more blood spilled this night!'

Hurting some yet ignoring the pain, Gabriel now stood in back of the altar with his six-gun at the ready with Carmelita safely in back of him. He wasn't certain if Vega would be heeded, considering the number of Moneros men out there. What he had no way of knowing was that during those final gunsmoke minutes horsemen with naked guns had stormed through the hacienda defences to gallop up to the very doors of the besieged chapel itself.

Marshal McTigue had arrived!

The hardcase lawman had made it at the eleventh hour in response to Ford's wire ... and now came storming in at the head of a full strength bunch of grim riders from the Cattleman's Association boosted by a scatter of local citizens – the formidable squad trailed sedately by an unarmed yet totally commanding Judge Osgood.

Despite the odds now swinging heavily in his favour, Ford realized that McTigue's appearance alone would prove sufficient to achieve control over the chaotic situation. He would never know one way or the other, for in that tumultuous instant with the relief riders surging into the chapel proper, brandishing guns, it was Antonio Vega himself who realized the day was lost.

Abruptly the haggard-eyed don dropped his gun and raised both hands ... and instantly a dozen relieved and beaten lesser men followed suit, while there was still time.

In mere moments the smoke-filled chapel fell quiet – and suddenly, amazingly, Don Antonio and his lady quietly and calmly began moving about attending to the injured.

Still with his Colt hanging at his side,

Gabriel watched with something like awe as he saw Carmelita rip up the skirt of her wedding gown to fashion swabs for the wounded, which included Ford, whose shallow bullet crease she eventually attended to personally.

He'd been in plenty of shooting scrapes in his time but due to its location and high emotion, this showdown-cum-aborted wedding had to be the most nerve-wracking and memorable.

The good padre had eventually passed out and sat slumped in his padded chair with one foot resting upon the dead Chantaro's chest, while Moneros lay exactly where he had fallen.

The padre had dropped his Bible. It lay open close to Gabriel's blood-spattered boots. He picked it up curiously and squinted a passage which read:

As the whirlwind passeth, so the wicked is no more; but the righteous is an everlasting foundation.

The whirlwind passeth...

He gazed around, nodded. It seemed to him the words just about summed it all up.

Out of the east burst the sun and the curtain

168

of night was lifted by the shafts of pink, white and gold all streaming across the skies in delicate trails of colour.

Ford Gabriel had seen many a sunrise but couldn't recall one like this. It was as though nature was intent on putting on her finest display to help the people of Coronado recover from the bloody events which had threatened to engulf the town during the night.

Sunlight warmly filled the courtyards of the Vega mansion and splashed across the adobe, frame, brick and timbers of the town crouched beside the big river.

Days like this the Rio Grande seemed to glory in its own extravagant grace and beauty and colour as it rolled timelessly by Coronado on its long journey to the sea.

When Carmelita went indoors to help with the breakfast, brother Rodrigo emerged to sit in silence upon the gallery's top step. His left arm had been broken but the medico had done a fine job setting and splinting. Even so the young Vega's injury would keep him out of action longer than Gabriel. Don Zebulon's slug had furrowed across Ford's back muscles but had not found bone. He would be stiff for a while, yet mobile.

After a silence, Rodrigo suddenly rem-

169

arked, 'My father put his arm around me this morning...'

Ford appeared puzzled. He didn't get the significance.

'He hasn't done that since I was a child,' Rodrigo explained. 'I doubt he *could* have done it ... before last night.' He looked up. 'He's changed ... like I feel all of us have. Maybe it is as they say, Gabriel? It's an ill wind that doesn't blow somebody some good.'

'Maybe.' Gabriel produced a cigar and looked at the town below. 'I'm planning to marry your sister, Rodrigo.'

'Are you asking ... or telling?'

'Telling.'

The handsome young Mexican almost smiled. 'So it seems that death and violence do not seem to leave much effect upon you, gringo.'

'We'll live poor but honest,' Ford went on. 'There is nothing you or anybody else can do about it.'

'Well, my father shall be pleased.'

'Sure. He'll throw a big party.'

'No, I mean this. You see, the *patrón* really has changed. Last night with all the bloodshed and death he finally came to realize what he'd become through greed and pride.

He is a humble man today. I believe he will welcome you as a son-in-law – poor and ill-mannered though you may he.' He winked. 'Who knows? Perhaps in time I may even accept you as a brother-in-law.'

'You mean that?'

The youth sobered and nodded. 'I believe I do.'

Gabriel eased as far back in his chair as he could without placing pressure on his back. Then, raising booted feet to the balustrade, he crossed them and settled back to reflect upon the great mystery of how people could change events, and how sometimes events changed people.

'It would have saved me one hell of a lot of trouble had we kept you down in Sharra-stone, Gabriel,' Marshal McTigue complained, red-eyed and heavy-footed after five days of investigation and paperwork at the Coronado jailhouse.

'You know you couldn't have done that, Marshal,' Gabriel said, poker-faced. 'It would have been against the law. You knew I was innocent.'

'Guessed,' McTigue corrected. 'Now, thanks to the Hacienda crew finally finding themselves in a position where they are free

171

to discuss Don Zebulon and all his illegal activities without fear for the first time, we finally know he planted that stolen horse on you a year back – just as we have proof he murdered both Buell and the rancher.'

'Thanks to me ... you know all that now.'

Gabriel was enjoying himself. The marshal had been characteristically thorough in his investigations and had absolved all survivors from blame in the aftermath of the events of that day which the river folk already referred to as Bloody Friday. Ford's wounds were healing nicely and he and Carmelita were well advanced with their wedding plans.

In truth, if he had one major concern now, it was the daunting prospect of seeking out a decent and well-paid job which would suit a married man better than busting his backside breaking wild horses.

'I have to agree ... thanks to you,' McTigue was willing to concede. 'I'll go further. I hate to admit it Gabriel, but not even a regular trained peace officer could have done a better job and shown more grit and gumption than you did in cleaning up the mess this town was in.'

Gabriel dropped his ribbing. He smiled. 'Thanks, Marshal. I only did what I had to.'

'Why?'

'What kind of question is that?'

'I'm interested in what exactly made you keep on doing what you knew had to be done?'

'It's a man's duty to do what he sees as right.'

'That's a good answer, Gabriel.'

'It is?'

'The best. On account it helps me make up my mind on something.' McTigue drew documents from his pocket. 'With three crooked law officials in jail here awaiting trial for corruption and dereliction of duty, and with me due to leave for the West on tomorrow morning's paddle steamer, suddenly I've got a problem. I want to leave someone in this here office who is both tough enough and dedicated enough to handle the sheriff's job.'

'Guess you do.'

McTigue extended his right hand and opened his fingers, and Gabriel saw the five-pointed star resting in his palm. He straightened sharply in puzzlement. The other wordlessly indicated the five-pointer then tapped Ford's chest with a question in his eyes. But Gabriel still didn't catch on until the other almost smiled for once in his life.

'How does Sheriff Gabriel on fifty dollars

a week plus fine fees sound?'

Gabriel couldn't believe just how fine it did sound. He knew he could handle such a job and instantly saw it as a serious possibility and something really worth while.

Yet some time later as he took his first walk through the streets of Coronado with the star on his chest, he couldn't help but slip into the old cocky swagger. He was congratulated by both friends and strangers, but was plainly so proud that Rodrigo Vega felt obliged to bring him back down to earth when he met him heading up Cedar Hill to carry the news to Carmelita.

'You know, it's only a job, Gabriel. There's no need to take it too big. That star doesn't mean you own Coronado, you know?'

He was right, Ford mused. He did not own Coronado. But that day it sure felt like he did.

The publishers hope that this book has given you enjoyable reading. Large Print Books are especially designed to be as easy to see and hold as possible. If you wish a complete list of our books please ask at your local library or write directly to:

Dales Large Print Books
Magna House, Long Preston,
Skipton, North Yorkshire.
BD23 4ND